FORCED TO FLEE FROM AN ARMED AND FURIOUS FOE

This was the most dangerous passage yet. It was low and narrow with a sliding gravel floor. The crabs had told them that the chamber was big enough for all of them, but they could not tell how big the next passage out of it would be, or if any existed at all.

Bones found himself sliding down wet gravel and rocks on his back, struggling to keep his feet from hitting Jackson's head and shoulders right below him. Then suddenly they spilled into a large chamber, and Bones lay on his back, looking up.

He got to his feet and moved close to a wall so that his headlamp shone directly on it. The wall was light brown with sedimentary strata running up at a sharp angle. Then he turned and looked at the shape of the entire cavern.

"I want to go down again," Bones said.

"That's crazy," said Jackson. "We're in a questionable spot already if you ask me."

"I'm on to something here. We have a fossil record that may be worth a great deal."

Books in the Dr. Bones series:

DR. BONES

BOOK 2

The Cosmic Bomber

William F. Wu

A BYRON PREISS VISUAL PUBLICATIONS, INC.
BOOK

iBooks
Habent Sua Fata Libelli

iBooks
Manhanset House
Dering Harbor, New York 11965
bricktower@aol.com • www.ibooksinc.com

Text, Illustrations, and Cover Artwork
Copyright © 1989 by Byron Preiss Visual Publications.
DR. BONES is a registered trademark of Byron Preiss Visual Publications
Developed by Byron Preiss and Paul Preuss.
Cover art by Jim Burns.
Visual data by Joel Hagen.
Character design by Steranko.
Edited by David M. Harris.
Series editor: Paul Preuss.
Special thanks to Mary H. Higgins, Susan Allison,
Beth Fleisher, and Gwendolyn Smith.

Library of Congress Cataloging-in-Publication Data
Wu, William F. Cosmic Bomber.
        (Dr. Bones) "A Byron Preiss Visual Publications Book."
p. cm.
        [1. Fiction—Science Fiction—Hard Science Fiction. 2. Fiction—
Science Fiction—Crime & Mystery. 3. Fiction—Science Fiction—Alien
Contact.] I. Hagen, Joel. ill. II. Title. III. Series: Dr. Bones.

ISBN 978-1-59687-943-0
January 2021

This novel is dedicated to:
Michael D. Toman
Medlo C. Steadman
and
Buck Milligan
all of whom survived across the prairies,
the plains, the Rockies, and the desert
to reach the sunlit shore.

ACKNOWLEDGMENTS

Special thanks are due to David M. Harris, Michael D. Toman, Rob Chilson, and Paul Preuss for their contributions in the creation of this novel.

The Cosmic Bomber

Table of Contents

Chapter One

Dr. Ezekiel Bones glanced down at the small clock imbedded in the corner of the podium in front of him as he went on talking. It was time to wrap up this lecture. Certainly his students wouldn't complain, no matter how interested in the subject they were.

"So that gives you the basics on the cometary-bombardment theory of evolutionary saltations," he said, glancing at the tiered rows of seats curving ahead of him. "That is, jumps in evolution." He switched off the prompter in the surface of the podium and tossed a full shock of wavy blond hair out of his eyes. "Are there any questions?"

"Dr. Bones?" A young man in the third row raised his hand.

"Yes."

"Does one major collision between a comet and a planet provide enough data to support this theory on that planet? Even if that one collision causes clear changes in the direction of the planet's evolution, one example is not much of a pattern."

"Yeah," said someone else. "What if something else caused the change in evolution and the timing was a coincidence?"

"That's possible. Good question." Zeke moved to the side of the podium and leaned casually on it. "Actually, a number of the planets that show evidence of at least one cometary bombardment also exhibit evidence of other collisions. Comets sometimes orbit in groups large enough to cause repeated collisions, as we believe happened on Earth a number of times."

The first student nodded. "So each of these planets usually gives you a number of examples. What about planets without cometary bombardment? Do they show less evolution?"

Zeke shook his head, giving the kid a broad grin. He liked students who really wanted to find out about something. "They don't necessarily show less evolutionary development. However, they definitely show fewer jumps from the supremacy of one form of life to another. They will usually give you evolutionary patterns that go in a straight line of descent. When these planets possess an evolutionary complexity comparable to that of planets with cometary saltations, they are much older planets—in the billions of years—and tend to be concentrated toward the center of the galaxy where everything is older."

He glanced around and called on a young woman up high in the last row.

"You presented this idea as a theory," she said. "Do you believe in it, Dr. Bones?" She cocked her head to one side, her short brown hair swaying as she waited for his answer.

"Yes, I do. Major changes in the direction of evolution have occurred on many planets after a major collision with a comet."

"But how many times does a collision occur without causing a change in evolutionary direction?" she asked.

"It depends on the impact of the collision. If the dust thrown into the air from the collision blocks out the sunlight for as long as a year or more, the major plants will suffer and the larger animals at the top of the food chain will be the most likely to go." He glanced at his watch. They had another minute or so.

"And what did you mean just now about the supremacy of one form of life giving way to another?" The same woman asked.

"When the large animals at the top of the food chain die in large numbers for lack of food, smaller animals have the advantage in survival and reproduction. As I mentioned earlier in my talk, small mammals on Earth superseded the dinosaurs after such a collision." He grinned. "Or did you sleep through that part?"

The class laughed good-naturedly.

"Dr. Bones?" It was the first student again.

"Yes, go ahead."

"You said that, in some cases, millions of years will pass between the collisions on a given planet."

"That's right."

"Why so long? If the planet and the comets are both on regular orbits, why don't they hit every orbit?"

Some of the other students laughed, but Zeke kept a straight face. "After one comet destroys itself by hitting a planet, the way may be clear for a long time before another comet works its way into a collision course. Even regular orbits aren't precisely exact, and the two bodies will spend most of their time in different parts of their orbits. It may take them millions of years to move from near misses to a hit." Zeke started to speak further, then noticed that his students were all looking off to the side, toward the doorway.

Sylvie Pharr stood leaning against the doorjamb, her arms folded, grinning at him.

Zeke grinned back at her. "Class dismissed," he called out, waving for the students to disperse.

Nobody moved.

Zeke jumped off the dais to meet Sylvie. She remained where she was, her step-cut triangle of black hair shining over her skin-tight red suit and glittering gold jewelry. All eyes in the auditorium were on her, but as an interplanetary correspondent, combat photographer, and colleague of Dr. Bones, she was not unused to attention.

She straightened up as he approached and the light glinted off her decorative metallic collars. They were solar collectors that powered her various recording devices, all incorporated into her outfit. Even her tiara doubled as an antenna for communications.

"How long have you been waiting here?" Zeke demanded, with a grin. "You should have spoken up. Why didn't you just call down from the *Ostrom*? You didn't have to leave orbit yourself."

"Jackson had an errand down here anyway. Besides, I didn't want to interrupt you during a lecture."

"That's silly," said Zeke. "You know you can call me and leave a message."

"Yes, I know." Sylvie laughed. "Zeke, I've seen you in all kinds of tight spots, but watching you handle questions out of left field is always entertaining. So you're talking about cometary bombardment, eh? After sending me off to investigate the situation on Thomsen 4?"

Zeke grinned. "I just figured I might as well get double use out of all the homework we had to do on the subject. Besides, it fits this class on evolutionary theories."

"I can't argue with that."

"Now, then. What did you find out?"

"Before I report . . . Are you aware that every student in the room is watching our every move?" She put a hand on her hip.

"Yeah, I know. I'm afraid Doc Bones is becoming legendary on this campus, whether I like it or not. And you're part of the legend." He shook his head in mock regret.

"Whether I like it or not. All right, I get it." Her voice took on a businesslike tone. "The Thomsen 4 situation is just as you guessed. Another comet is on a collision course with it, right on schedule according to its past bombardments, as far as we know of them."

"And someone has plans to divert it?"

"I think so," said Sylvie. "If so, it's probably some corporate developer. I have feelers out now to identify the exact owner, but they haven't reported yet."

"That's all we need to know for now," said Zeke, nodding thoughtfully. "A developer wants to save the planet and then move in. No one is going to watch out for its native peoples. Did you confirm that a sentient race is native to the planet?"

"Sort of."

"What?"

"A species called the Arrs is considered sentient by some experts, but not by all," said Sylvie. "Frankly, we don't know much about them or the planet."

"You mean that's it?"

"Almost. I have some more details on file on the *Ostrom*." She shrugged apologetically. "It's too recent a discovery and not enough visits have been made to provide more data."

"Again, that's close enough. We'll have to find out for ourselves." He gently turned her. "Come on, let's go see if I can get some time off from the department head."

As they walked away, the students finally left their seats and exited the hall. A number of them followed Zeke and Sylvie down the corridor at a discreet distance, talking excitedly among themselves.

"Really, Zeke," said Sylvie. "Do you think there's any change you can't get leave?"

"Well . . ." He winked at her. "I'm leaving, period. The question is, will I be welcome back? I haven't been a very reliable lecturer, with all the running around we've been doing lately."

"I don't think they'd dare do without you."

"We'll soon find out. In the meantime, what about the team? Have you assembled everyone?"

"Marty and Kadak!xa are on board the *Ostrom* in orbit right now. Reelys had to send his'er regrets."

"And my ol' buddy Jackson Charles?"

"I brought Jackson down from orbit with me and dropped him off. He's visiting an elite art gallery in a resort area—the Ozark Mountains, I think it was. The lander has it on computer. We'll pick him up before we return to the *Ostrom*."

"The Ozarks? Why didn't he take the other lander down himself?"

"We aren't in a hurry, so we can save a little fuel this way."

Den Tanaka, the department head, was just leaving his office as they reached it. The tall, slender man took one look at the two of them and rolled his eyes. "Oh, no, Zeke . . . Not again."

"Hey, Den, I haven't even had a chance to speak yet."

Den sighed. "All right, all right. How are you, Sylvie?"

"Fine, Den. But we have a favor to ask. Can I have him for a little while?"

"Can I stop you?" He shook his head, smiling wistfully. "I wish I could run off any time I felt like it. What is it this time?"

"A planet called Thomsen 4," said Zeke.

Den turned around again and opened the door to his office. "Come on in." He motioned for them to enter.

"Thomsen 4 is the only planet that supports life in a young solar system," said Zeke.

They entered Den's office. The door closed behind them, but they remained standing.

"A new biosphere," said Den. "And you want to get in on the beginning to study it?"

"There's a lot more to it than that, Den." Zeke shook his head. "The planet has a history of cometary bombardment and another comet is on a collision course with it."

"A collision course, eh? And you want to study the effects of the collision on the life forms?"

"Den, will you stop jumping ahead of me? If it strikes, it'll wipe out a new sentient race that has evolved on Thomsen 4. Or at least, some people believe they are sentient. We can find out. They deserve a chance in any case."

"It so happens," Sylvie interjected, "that we think a corporate developer is making plans to divert the comet."

"Then what's the problem? Why do they need Zeke Bones out there to help?"

"I haven't verified the plans to divert it," said Sylvie. "If it's just a rumor, then we'll have to do it."

"Even if the rumor is true," said Zeke, "we might be able to help. Most importantly, though, I want to be on hand when the developer moves onto the surface of the planet after the comet has been diverted."

"I get it." Den sighed. "You want to watchdog the treatment of the native species. Right?"

"You got it, Den." Zeke grinned. "You finally got it right. What do you say?"

"I know better than to try talking you out of it. That's for sure." Den moved to his secretary's empty cubicle and pressed the computer voicecon. "Computer, page Prof. Lois Thurman. Request her presence here as soon as possible."

"Thanks, Den." Zeke offered his hand and shook with him.

"I must be crazy. Look, I was just going to have lunch. My secretary has already gone. Do you two have time to join me?"

"Sure," said Sylvie, with a glance at Zeke. "We have a long trip ahead. No sense consuming more shipboard food than we have to."

"Where to?" Zeke asked, as they left the office again.

"My usual. It's a little sandwich place with an outdoor patio overlooking a run-down warehouse area."

"Getting your revenge now, eh?" Zeke nudged him with his elbow and laughed.

The view was not nearly as bad as Den had implied. They sat on a patio in the shade of an umbrella, overlooking a curving boulevard roughly a story below. Across from it, and beyond a wide green lawn, Zeke could just see the edge of a warehouse district.

After finishing lunch, he leaned back and let the breeze ruffle his hair.

"I'll call Jackson with our ETA," said Sylvie. "He'll appreciate the courtesy."

"I hate to hurry," said Zeke. "It's comfortable here. Still, that comet closing in on Thomsen 4 won't wait."

"I'm glad you approve," said Den.

Sylvie rolled her eyes. "Hates to hurry, he says. Zeke, I've seen you rush around galaxies more frantically than anyone. When your blood is up, you won't stay still for a minute."

Zeke shrugged. "I like my leisure, too."

"No kidding!" A woman yelled behind Zeke. "What about the rest of us, *Doctor* Bones?"

Zeke turned to see a short, dark-haired woman striding resolutely toward him. "Hi, Lois."

"Don't you 'Hi, Lois' me, you parasite!"

"Hey, easy, Lois." Zeke frowned in surprise.

"Everybody else here carries a full load. It's time you started shouldering your own burden for a change."

"Uh—"

"How 'bout it, Zeke?" Lois demanded.

Sylvie glanced at Zeke with an amused smile.

"Wait a minute," said Den. "I'm the one who paged you, Lois. And I haven't even made my request yet."

Lois whirled on him. "You paged me, all right! You told me to come to your office and then you left! Thank *you*, Mr. Tanaka."

"We were short of time," Den said lamely.

"And what about this request of yours—are you going to tell me I'm wrong? You're going to ask me to finish his lecture responsibilities again this term, aren't you?"

"Uh—well . . ." Den smiled weakly and shrugged.

"You sniveling coward. Who really runs our department, anyway?" She glared at both of them.

Zeke glanced at Den, a trifle embarrassed.

"Lois, you know Zeke has an unusual arrangement with this institution," Den said patiently. "I don't—"

"That's no excuse! Whatever arrangement he has—*you* have, Zeke, you have no right to take on responsibilities and then abandon them unfinished."

"I didn't know this would come up, Lois," said Zeke, sitting up in his chair.

"But you certainly knew that *something* would come up! Something always comes up where you're concerned!"

"Well . . . I guess it looks that way." Zeke sighed.

"Lois," Den said firmly. "*I* paged you, not Zeke. Suppose you take it up with me."

"Ha! Suppose I take it up with both of you. Or better yet, suppose I refuse outright."

"I have to find someone to take over his spot," said Den. "You're the best qualified."

"Except for you, Den. Why don't *you* take over his spot?" Lois stood over him with her hands on her hips.

Zeke stifled a grin. "Sylvie, maybe we should get moving after all. That comet—"

"It won't arrive in the next few minutes," said Sylvie. "You can relax here for a minute more."

"Thanks a lot."

"Den," said Lois, with a trace of a sneer. "Why *don't* you take over his lectures?"

"Maybe you should go with my team," said Zeke. "I could stay and take over your classes."

Lois turned to him with an exaggerated expression of approval.

"Well, there's an idea. Maybe you should stay."

"It's always exciting out there," said Sylvie.

"I'll bet that's true." Lois glanced at her and then back at Zeke. "I've done some fieldwork on other planets."

"We're diverting a comet," said Sylvie. "It's about to collide with a planet that has a newly developed sentient life form."

Lois hesitated. "You're diverting a comet?"

"It's always exciting where Zeke goes," said Den impishly. "So we all hear, anyway."

"And after that," Zeke added, "we'll have to watchdog a corporate developer and make sure that the natives aren't simply shoved aside. Their young culture is in a very fragile stage."

"That's more like it," said Lois. "At least it's real field-work in the discipline."

"There won't be any native culture to protect if the comet hits," said Sylvie. "Zeke?"

"We should be going," said Zeke, rising. "Lois, would you like to go some time?"

She blinked in surprise. "Me?"

"You're right that I have many demands on me. Another project will come along soon, provided I take care of this one properly. If we plan ahead, and you're interested, you could go."

"Are you serious?" She demanded suspiciously.

"Yes, of course." He shrugged apologetically. "You understand that this time we already have a team assembled. But next time, if you were free to go . . ."

She looked at Den. "I'd have to get leave myself, wouldn't I? From you."

"Zeke," Sylvie said firmly.

"Coming."

"And to get leave next time, I'll have to be on your good side, won't I, Den?" Lois shook her head in ironic disgust. "All right, Zeke, have it your way. You're pretty slick."

"Thanks, Lois. Bye, Den." Zeke waved to both of them and hurried after Sylvie.

"And Dr. Bones escapes again," said Sylvie, laughing quietly when they were out of hearing.

"The trouble is, she's right," said Zeke. "I'll have to make it up to her some other time. For now, let's get out of here!"

Chapter Two

Zeke piloted the winged lander into a sharp ascent, then turned over the flying to the computer. The distance from New Yale University to a high society hideaway in the Ozark Mountains was not significant to a lander like this, but navigating through the low mountain range to the right inlet on the Lake of the Ozarks might require some attention. He kept an eye on the various readouts.

"Is Lois a friend?" Sylvie asked. "She appears capable and aggressive, just the way you like your friends."

"I like to think of her as a friend, but I don't know her very well."

"She was pretty angry, wasn't she?"

"Yeah, that was unfortunate but unavoidable. Basically, you just caused a billiard ball effect."

"What do you mean?"

"You knocked my routine out of orbit, so to speak, and in turn I knocked her routine out of orbit. We're all bouncing around just like the celestial bodies I was lecturing on."

"How quaint."

Zeke glanced at one of the screens casually, then did a double take. "Sylvie."

She instantly turned businesslike at his tone. "What is it?" She sat up.

"Do you have any reason to believe someone might be following us? I think we've picked up a tail." Zeke studied the screen thoughtfully. "It swung into position after we were in the air. It didn't come from New Yale."

"I don't know of any reason we should have a tail," said Sylvie. "Shall I hail them?"

"Go ahead. Maybe it's just a coincidence."

"Now hailing."

Zeke was glad he had discarded his casual lecture clothes for his traveling outfit. He was once again wearing his black vest jacket with the white piping on the seams and pockets, his matching pants, and black boots. His chrome belt, shoulder armor, and helmet fitting were still stashed away, but he might just want to put them on before landing.

"No response, Zeke," said Sylvie. "Still hailing, but they've had plenty of time."

"Meaning they don't want to talk to us."

"Looks that way."

"Alert Jackson and the *Ostrom* to be on the lookout. I'm going to put on my gear."

"Right."

Zeke stood up, though stooped over in the cramped lander, and took out the rest of his gear. He donned the shoulder armor, the trusted piece of equipment remaining from his old days in the Legion of Ares. Then he snapped together his distinctive "Doc Bones" belt buckle with his stylized Jolly Roger logo. The reference from old pirate tales was ironic; at times his opponents seemed more like pirates to him. Still, it symbolized his independence of action when he descended upon unscrupulous raiders.

He decided he wouldn't need the helmet.

Behind him, Sylvie had made contact.

"Jackson? Sylvie. Zeke and I are coming in on schedule. We think we've picked up a tail—no, no i.d. or hint of intentions. No hostility yet, either. Just be aware . . . Marty, are you there, too? You read? Fine. Lander out."

Zeke slid back into the pilot's chair. "All clear, I take it?"

"All clear. We're the only ones with company."

"Or we're the only ones who have noticed it."

They remained silent for a while. Zeke observed that the following craft kept a discreet distance and occasionally seemed to veer away or drop back out of sight. However, it always returned.

Finally the lander entered a sharp descent. As the white clouds broke around it, Zeke could see the bright and dark green ridges of the Ozark Mountains fast approaching. Then the sprawling, many-fingered Lake of the Ozarks came into view.

"Assuming manual control," said Zeke. "Sylvie, keep an eye on our friend."

"He's dropping back."

Zeke got the exact landing site from the computer and looked for it below. The lake sprawled, sending many fingers out between the various ridges and mountains surrounding it. Finally he found a configuration that matched their destination. "Sylvie, is that the strip there? See it on the right?"

"That's it, right alongside the lake. The Featherwing Art Gallery is that large building on the bluff above it."

"Okay. So we need a sharp descent beyond that ridge toward the water, leveling out just over the lake and maximum deceleration on the strip."

Sylvie laughed. "That's what I did when I dropped him off."

"Okay, okay. Just checking." Zeke grinned and sent the lander into a dive that left Sylvie gasping and grabbing for a handhold. "Clear us for landing."

Sylvie contacted the strip. "All clear to land. I've reserved a parking spot right on the strip, since we won't be here long."

"Here we go." Zeke watched the surface of the big lake grow, then deftly leveled out to skim over the small waves.

"We're naked again, boss man."

"Eh?" Zeke glanced up at her sarcastic tone.

"We lost our tail when we dropped through the cloud layer. Not for long, I suspect."

"I think you're right. Coming in."

The lander sped briefly over water and then took position to land on a strip that ran parallel to the lakeshore along the edge of the water. Zeke brought it in smoothly to a stop.

A few moments later they climbed out of the lander and looked around. Blue-green water lapped the edge of the strip. Some small boats were tied there, a john boat and some other open boats with outboard motors, apparently used for fishing. Across the narrow finger of water, green forest rose up over another ridge.

"What are those antiques doing here?" Zeke stopped to look. "I haven't seen motors like that since I went to a gallery show on primitive technology."

"For leisure," said Sylvie. "People like old technology on water."

"Of course. Like sailboats, canoes . . ."

"There's a lift over here," said Sylvie, plucking at his arm. "It rides straight up the side of the bluff to the gallery."

"All right." Zeke was squinting up into the sky. "It's peaceful here, isn't it?"

He followed her into a small transparent booth and they rode up the side of the bluff. His spine prickled, but not with the height. "We're totally exposed here."

"Easy, Doc. Nobody's shooting at us."

"That's the only reason I got inside this thing in the first place. Still, until I know who was following us and why, we should stay on alert. We'll go back down another way."

At the top of the bluff, the rear wall of the lift opened onto a tiled patio along one side of the gallery. Sylvie started for a side door, but Zeke stopped her.

"He's up there."

At the back of the patio, a wide set of steps led up to a veranda that opened on the side of the gallery's second story, toward the rear. Jackson Charles, all two black muscular meters of him, sat on the stone wall of the veranda. He wore his usual gray fatigues with olive trim.

As Zeke and Sylvie approached, Jackson was gazing across the lake stroking his short beard, the sunlight shining on his bald head. No one else was on the veranda.

"Jackson!" Zeke waved and trotted up the steps, aware of Sylvie right behind him.

"Zeke." Jackson grinned. "This is quite a place. Quiet, serene . . . It takes money to hang out here, though. I can see that just by looking around."

"Any sign of trouble?" Zeke asked.

"No, nothing. In fact . . ." Jackson nodded toward the interior of the gallery, through two large open doorways.

Inside, a small group of well-dressed visitors milled casually among the hanging paintings and sculptures on pedestals.

"Every time I walk inside, the crowd parts before me." He shrugged his broad shoulders.

Zeke laughed and clapped him on the back. "It's not the first time, as I recall."

"You just plain look too tough," said Sylvie. "*We* know how gentle and educated you are, but you still scare strangers."

Jackson shook his head. "Don't I know it. And all I was doing was looking at the artwork."

"Did you find anything from Thomsen 4?" Sylvie asked.

"No."

"Why? What's up?" Zeke asked.

"Our information is spotty, but there is someone on Thomsen 4 right now who is connected with a certain developer interested in the planet. In the past, she has provided this gallery with art and we wanted to see if any looting had occurred."

"Maybe they're clean, and maybe they just haven't had time to get any loot here," said Jackson. "Either way, I've been through everything on display."

"Did you check the acquisitions on them?" Zeke asked. "Is it all Earth art or does it include other planets?"

"It's almost all from Earth." Jackson glowered. "Of course I checked. And I'm happy to say that they were all legally acquired."

"Maybe so," Zeke said doubtfully. "The people they bought from may not have been so careful."

"We have a moment to go inside and look around," said Sylvie. "I'll record anything questionable on the sly."

"Sure." Jackson stood up and gestured. "Lead the way."

Zeke hesitated, then reluctantly followed them into the gallery. The other patrons glanced at Jackson towering above Sylvie and Zeke and discreetly moved down adjacent aisles. Zeke shook his head, grinning, and stopped in front of an elaborate piece of sculpture.

"Abstract?" Sylvie asked.

"No way," said Jackson, coming up beside her on the other side. "That's a realist piece from the Harmony System."

"Harmony 9," said Zeke, nodding. "It's a rendition of a certain plant the natives once held sacred. The religion has evolved away from that, but they still hold it in high regard."

"There's an interesting piece over there," said Jackson, pointing down the aisle.

"I'll take your word for it," said Zeke. "I'm sorry to cut this short, but if you've checked in here, I think we better get up to the *Ostrom*. Whoever followed up here wants something and won't say what. We're too vulnerable down here."

Jackson nodded. "Agreed."

The three of them walked purposefully out the side doors onto the veranda. Zeke started to turn toward the stairs but stopped at the sight of Jackson as he winced in pain, spun, and fell to the tiled veranda floor.

"Jackson?" Sylvie said, puzzled.

"Down!" Zeke yelled, crouching behind the low wall of the veranda.

"What is it?" she asked.

He reached back to take Sylvie's wrist and pull her down.

Jackson, still grimacing, rolled over and looked around.

Sylvie was recording sight and sound in all directions, switching on the jewelry she wore that doubled as sensors. Then she contacted the *Ostrom* and reported that they were under attack.

"How bad?" Zeke asked, still looking at the forest across the water. "I don't see anything."

"I'm not hurt bad," said Jackson. "It was a sonic gun. The vibrations just caught my side, but most of it missed."

Zeke stared into the breeze from the lake, searching for a hint of snipers somewhere in the trees across the narrow finger of water. He saw nothing. "And we're totally un-armed."

Vibrations struck one of bricks next to his head, the sound waves coming in at a range the human ear could not detect. The mortar below the brick cracked. Dust blew away in the breeze, and the brick slid slightly out of place.

Beside Zeke, Sylvie crawled on her elbows up next to him. "See anything?"

He shook his head. "We have to move," he said. "They have us measured, and we can't even see them."

Inside the gallery, voices were shouting excitedly. Someone would undoubtedly be calling the authorities.

"A sonic gun doesn't flash," muttered Zeke. "If they're well hidden, we won't see anything from here."

"The lander's in plain sight," said Sylvie. "If they think of it, they can take it out of action and strand us here."

"No." Zeke shook his head, firing again. "The guns they're using aren't strong enough. Must be hand weapons with a wide focus. Jackson, are you up to a little running?"

"Whenever you say."

The unseen enemy fired again, and panes shattered in the gallery doors behind them. Patrons inside screamed.

"We gotta go," said Zeke. "We're endangering the gallery and everyone in here."

"Where to?" Sylvie asked.

"If we run, he'll just keep shooting. We'll have to go after him," called Zeke.

"You sure you want to try that?" She demanded.

"Come on!" Jackson yelled. Holding his side with one hand, he leaped past Zeke and Sylvie to run down the steps.

Sylvie followed, running low. Zeke brought up the rear. Sonic vibrations greater than before tore away chunks of the stone bannister as he ran past.

Ahead, Jackson was half-climbing and half-sliding down a crevice in the steep slope. It led back to the landing strip and the water's edge. He was completely exposed to the sonic fire that vibrated chunks of earth and rock loose over his head. Finally he reached the bottom and flopped down heavily, prone on the lake edge.

Now Sylvie made her descent. Zeke was sure by this time that only one sniper was firing at them and he was a lousy shot. Rushing him was worth the risk.

Sylvie threw herself to the ground next to Jackson.

Finally Zeke scooted down the nearly vertical slope. By the time he was running to join the others, they were in one of the small boats tied at the water's edge. Jackson was just firing up the outboard motor.

Zeke cast off the line and jumped in. The boat rocked crazily as Jackson twisted the motor into gear and they took off for the opposite shore in a fine white spray.

Suddenly Zeke felt hard vibrations jar the armor on his shoulder, knocking him onto his back in the bottom of the boat.

"Zeke?" Sylvie called, over the roar of the motor.

Zeke worked his shoulder experimentally. "Not serious. Between the armor and our erratic route, it didn't hit squarely."

Jackson killed the engine several meters from shore, before the propellor ran aground. Again grimacing in pain, he swung his legs out, splashed his heavy boots into the shallow water, and slogged toward the shore.

Zeke climbed out of the boat and followed Jackson.

Jackson and Zeke reached the shore about twelve meters apart. Zeke couldn't actually tell if the sniper was still shooting, since the vibrations were silent and their effect on the surface of the lake was not visible to the eye. Sylvie waded after them to the shore.

All three of them advanced low to the ground until they were protected by trees.

No fire came from the forested slope above them. The forest was dense here, with visibility of only about six meters.

Zeke wanted to capture the sniper alive if possible. He had to find out who was attacking them and why. He motioned for the other two to remain where they were.

The sniper had either fled or was lying in wait for them to expose themselves recklessly. At this close distance, his sonic gun would be more dangerous. Zeke began to crawl through the underbrush as quietly as he could.

Zeke's shoulder was feeling stiff but he knew he was not injured seriously. Still, it hindered his movements and made him noisier than he might have been. He stopped to listen and heard nothing.

He turned and waved for both Jackson and Sylvie to move up from their positions. When he drew no response, he started moving up again himself.

Before long, all three of them had reached the level where Zeke had estimated the sniper to be. After waiting a few more minutes, he took a deep breath and cautiously rose. Jackson and Sylvie also stood up slowly.

Just as Zeke began to relax, a movement to his left caught his eye. The sniper was bringing up his sonic hand weapon. Zeke started to duck and felt a surge of adrenalin as he realized that he was too late.

Instantly, Jackson leaped across the short expanse of brush and took down the sniper. They rolled over once, and then the sniper lay still.

Jackson got up cautiously and rolled the sniper over with his foot. "He's dead."

Zeke and Sylvie joined Jackson over the body.

"His weapon must have gone off when I hit him," said Jackson. "I wanted him alive."

"Couldn't be helped," said Zeke. "Thank you. Anyone recognize the outfit?"

"No," said Jackson.

"I'm recording everything," said Sylvie. "But I don't recognize anything. That's an ordinary sonic gun."

The sniper had a nondescript face with short brown hair. He wore a khaki jumpsuit and black boots. Nothing about him seemed remarkable at all.

Sylvie knelt by the body and emptied his few pockets. Nothing added a clue to his identity.

Zeke shook his head. "All right. Let's get back to the *Ostrom* right away."

Chapter Three

Zeke turned from the body of the sniper and started down the slope toward the water. "Come on, let's go. He can't help us now."

"Zeke," Jackson said quietly.

"Yeah?"

"His ship must be nearby. It might just tell us who's behind all this and why."

"It won't take long," said Sylvie.

"All right. Let's go." Zeke grinned at his own over-eagerness as he turned again. "You're right. I just doubt anything incriminating will be found there. I hate to waste time here when something's going on that must involve Thomsen 4."

They started up the slope. At times Zeke's single-mindedness could be overdone, he knew. He was just anxious to get out into space where the real problem lay.

When they crossed the crest of the ridge, they could see the sniper's ship through the trees. It was a small lander like their own, floating calmly on pontoons at the edge of another inlet of the lake. The entry had been left open. They hiked down the slope cautiously to the perimeter of the trees.

"I've been monitoring," said Sylvie quietly. "The ship hasn't been in contact with anyone. I've been hailing them, but they haven't answered."

They waited a few moments.

"No communications," Sylvie reported.

Zeke nodded and darted out of the forest toward the ship in a zigzag route, still anticipating enemy fire. He could hear Jackson doing the same, behind him and off to one side. Finally they met at the open entry ramp to the lander.

Jackson took a deep breath, then ran up the ramp. Inside, he planted himself and looked in all directions. Then he relaxed.

"It's empty, Zeke."

Zeke came up behind him and looked around. Then he punched into the ship computer.

"It's totally stripped down," said Jackson. "No personal items anywhere."

"No computer data to speak of, either," said Zeke. "Just standard navigational information. Not even a record of where the lander came from or what mother ship it belongs to."

"This lander is a Hannibal 614," said Jackson. "Standard model, very common."

"Zeke," Sylvie called, as she came up the ramp.

"Yeah?"

"The gallery authorities are calling. They have some questions about the firelight."

"So do we," Zeke muttered. "Like, why did that sniper miss us when he had so many opportunities?" He sighed. "All right, let's get back there. Tell 'em we're on our way."

"Get in, Sylvie," said Jackson. "I can drive this thing along the water back to the gallery. Someone else can pick up that little boat we borrowed."

"Let's do it," said Zeke.

Jackson sat down at the controls and closed the entry. The lander was much like their own, except for pontoons. Jackson taxied down the inlet and turned around the point of land toward the finger of water they had madly crossed while they had been under attack.

As they drew near the landing strip, Zeke could see the gallery patrons lining the veranda. Much of the action had been out of their sight. Still, they apparently had been watching what they could after the initial attack got their attention.

Jackson brought the lander alongside the landing strip. As they got out, the lift was descending from the gallery with several uniformed guards. Their expressions were grim; obviously, they expected an explanation.

Zeke got out first, closely followed by Jackson and Sylvie. He waited for the guards to approach, making clear to them that he was not in any hurry to get away on legal grounds.

One of the guards was a burly fellow nearly Zeke's height. He was flanked by two others who kept glancing uncomfortably over Zeke's shoulder. Jackson would be standing there.

Zeke knew from experience that Jackson had assumed his reserved and formal manner. At his size, that could be intimidating to watch. It sometimes gave the Bones team a useful psychological advantage, and they could use one now.

"What happened here, sir?" the first guard asked.

"I'm Dr. Ezekiel Bones," said Zeke. "I came here to pick up a colleague and we were attacked on your gallery veranda by a sniper from across the lake."

"And?" The guard demanded. "Exactly what are you doing here?"

"Wait a minute, wait a minute," called a voice behind him.

The guards turned around. A gray-haired man in civilian clothes was hurrying forward. "Dr. Bones? I did hear you say you're Dr. Bones, didn't I?"

"Yes, you did. And yes, I am."

"I'm Harold Prinz, curator of the gallery. Did you say a sniper attacked you?"

"That's right," Zeke took the man's offered hand and shook it. "He's dead now, killed accidentally when we were defending ourselves. This is his lander."

"Well, I certainly will take your word that it was an accident. I know of your reputation, of course. Can we do anything to help?"

Zeke grinned and spoke in a confidential manner. "To tell you the truth, we need to get out into space. Whoever sent the sniper down here has business with us out in another star system."

"The police will need to fill out a report," Prinz pointed out. "After all, a man is dead."

"Some poor pawn of the real enemy." Zeke nodded. "That's the tragedy."

"He was trying to kill you, after all. Perhaps if you could just wait a short time for the police? I have to think of the gallery, you know."

"Of course you must."

"You and your crew . . . you're off to another big adventure?"

"I like to think of it as a project. However, the faster we move on, the faster we'll draw snipers like this after us . . . and away from your gallery."

Prinz nodded slowly. He seemed to like being taken into the confidence of the famous Dr. Bones. "That is a consideration for the gallery, isn't it? How can I help?"

"Have your guards take custody of this lander and call the authorities. The local authorities will have to record the death of the sniper and take care of the other legal paperwork. Have them contact me through New Yale University and I'll arrange for them to have all the depositions they need at a later time."

"Be glad to," said Prinz. "You don't mind if we keep this out of the papers? For the sake of the gallery, you understand."

"Of course." Zeke shook his hand again. "Thank you, Mr. Prinz. We won't forget this."

"A pleasure meeting you, Dr. Bones."

Jackson turned and led the way back up into the lander. They closed the door and let out sighs of relief in near unison. Waiting for the local authorities to arrive, retrieve the body, and question them would have meant a long delay.

"Sylvie, will you do the honors?" Zeke asked, as he and Jackson collapsed into seats. "You're the only one who's unhurt."

"Glad to." Sylvie took the controls and brought the lander into position. Then she accelerated the lander and in a moment they were rising sharply from the strip, just in time to angle up over the next prominent ridge.

"Anyone following us?" Zeke asked. "Just in case that sniper had a partner in another lander."

"No sign of anything like that so far," said Sylvie. She turned over the flight to the computer, with orders to rendezvous with the *Ostrom*. Then she swung around to face the others. "It's more likely that the mother ship will pick us up in orbit, I would say."

Meanwhile, Jackson was examining his injured side. His outfit was pulled back to reveal the wound.

"How serious is it?" Zeke asked.

"Not very. It hurt at the time, but I think it's just going to be some deep bruises." Jackson grit his teeth as he poked at the injured area. "I don't think it even broke the skin."

"Good."

"I don't get it, Zeke," said Jackson, still studying his wound. "It doesn't make any sense."

"You don't get what?"

"Why would he use a small sonic gun at that distance? He hardly had a chance to kill anybody. The focus was too wide and dissipated over the distance involved."

"A couple of reasons," Zeke said grimly. "For one, he may have been hoping that the water would help hold the focus together. More important, though, I don't think he planned to try this here. We caught him off guard."

"What? Where, then?"

"I think he meant to hit me at New Yale," said Zeke. "He would have had crowds of people around. His small sonic gun can be hidden in a pocket."

Jackson nodded thoughtfully. "All right. At the frequencies he was using, the beam from it is quiet and invisible."

"Right," said Zeke. "He was counting on getting close to me in the crowd and then losing himself in it again. That also explains why he kept missing. He probably wasn't used to a small handgun."

"Now that makes sense," said Jackson. "He was an excellent shot with it, even so—almost got us even across the water. But why carry only one kind of weapon?"

"If he was pursued, he could ditch one weapon more easily than a couple of them." Zeke grinned. "Or maybe he was either stupid or cheap. Either way, we lucked out."

"No kidding," said Sylvie, who had finished her communications. "Our timing was perfect. I happened to get you out of New Yale just before he landed, so he tailed us from there."

"We still don't know why he would bother," said Zeke. "Sylvie, I know the basic situations on Thomsen 4, but I need the full briefing. What's behind all this?"

"Yeah," said Jackson. "Where is Thomsen 4, anyway?"

"The Thomsen system is on the fringe of human space," said Sylvie. "A long way from the borders of alien space."

Zeke nodded. "So alien intervention isn't likely."

"No."

"Thomsen," said Jackson. "That hasn't been part of known space very long, has it?"

Sylvie shook her head. "We have data on the planet from a couple of visits, but not very much."

Zeke ran a hand through his tousled hair. "Let me guess. An Earth-class planet, around one-gee gravity. That's why a developer is interested in it."

"That's right. And it has recently developed intelligent life from a lupoid species that is still in a primitive cultural stage. Or at least, that's one opinion."

"What's the other one?" Jackson asked.

"Well, some researchers don't feel that sentience has been proven yet. Remember, the data is absolutely minimal."

"Hmm." Zeke shook his head. "I don't like the sound of that. If a developer has authorities to testify that no sentient life is native to the planet, then people will be that much more comfortable shoving the natives out of the place like animals."

"I suppose they could be right," said Sylvie. "No one has proof either way."

"We'll see for ourselves," said Jackson. "Maybe we'll just get that proof."

"Lupoids," said Zeke thoughtfully. "Similar to wolves of Earth. Do they live in forests, then, or what?"

Sylvie nodded. "They live in a vast forested region in a temperate zone. There aren't very many of them, really, and they haven't spread to all of the inhabitable areas available to them."

"Why is a developer interested?" Jackson asked. "Is it just the Earth-normal similarity? Or is there more?"

"The planet bears a wealth of minerals, especially metals and potential fossil fuels, that will make developing it very easy," Sylvie said.

"That has at least as much to do with it," Zeke agreed.

A tone beeped on the console. Sylvie swung around instantly to check the readouts.

Zeke and Jackson also leaned forward to look.

"Nothing serious," said Sylvie. "We're joining more space traffic coming in and out of Earth orbit."

"Just watch 'em," growled Jackson. "One of them could still be another tail."

"And the sniper's mother ship must be out here somewhere," said Sylvie. "We'll have all our neighbors tracked."

"Take evasive action," said Zeke. "I want to see if any of them notice us."

"All right." Sylvie took the lander off computer and settled in at the controls. "Hang on."

Suddenly the lander veered away sharply, throwing Zeke's injured shoulder against the side wall. He winced and straightened into a better position. A moment later, she took the lander into a forward roll and he flailed for an extra restraining strap.

"Got one," called Sylvie.

"What is it?" Zeke asked.

"Looks like another winged lander to me. It broke out of its orbit to follow us."

"Get me the exact dimensions," said Jackson.

Sylvie punched in an order and a close-up of the lander in question appeared on the screen.

"Looks like another Hannibal 614 to me," said Jackson. "Probably no better armed than this lander is."

"Let's see what else it does," said Zeke.

"What do you mean?" Sylvie asked.

"Take us into another roll and head right for it. We'll take the initiative and see if they run or fight or what."

"You got it."

The lander angled up and to the right this time. Zeke and Jackson were fully strapped in and ready. The partial loop reversed their direction suddenly.

When the other lander was centered in their viewscreen, Sylvie leveled out. A second later, the other lander veered away sharply. She punched an order for the computer to track and follow it.

"You were right," said Sylvie to Jackson. "They don't look armed. They'd rather run than fight."

"Let's follow them for a little bit," said Zeke.

"Shall I have the computer project their route?" Sylvie asked.

"No, don't bother. We'll record the kind of evasive moves they make and leave it at that."

"Yeah," said Jackson. "They can't be dumb enough to lead us anywhere worth going to."

"We've given this long enough," said Zeke. "Let's get back to the *Ostrom*."

"Consider it done." Sylvie took another moment with the computer, then turned back to them. "They've gone their own way. It'll take us a little longer to dock with the *Ostrom* now, though."

"No problem," said Zeke with a grin. "Now on with the briefing."

"The geological studies are only a little more extensive than the rest of the data," said Sylvie.

"But the information about comets is sound?" Jackson asked.

"Yes," said Sylvie. "Marty has all the precise data on the *Ostrom* computer. That includes astronomical data of some comets in the Thomsen System that have been observed."

"So cometary bombardment has been repeated over the entire history of the planet," said Zeke. "Just as I was telling my students. If it weren't for the danger, I could have brought one or two on this project as a field trip." He smiled ironically.

"A comet of major size is now on a collision course with Thomsen 4," Sylvie continued. "It's orbit—"

"How major?" Jackson interrupted.

"I don't have the exact dimensions, but it is certain to cause widespread destruction. You can get the particulars from Marty after we dock."

"All right. Go ahead."

"We fully expect the collision to throw up a cloud of dust that will persist in the atmosphere." She looked at both Zeke and Jackson, giving a kind of shrug. "That's the crux of the matter."

"But for how long?" Zeke asked. "And how dense will it be? These questions make a big difference, too."

"We have no way of knowing. Not only is the angle of impact impossible to calculate precisely; we also don't know enough about the exact composition of the planet's crust. We know the usual makeup of comets, but even that is just a probability. We haven't had time to study this one in particular."

Zeke leaned back and nodded. "Of course. It could strike directly and smash the entire comet, or glance off at an angle, causing a lesser collision. And the dust cloud could be thick or thin, depending on the substances in it."

"So," said Jackson. "Since we can't predict the exact density of the dust cloud, we can't predict its exact duration, either."

"Or the extent of the damage," said Sylvie.

"But the danger to the lupoids is still clear?" Zeke asked.

She nodded. "They feed primarily on large herbivores in the forests I told you about. Those herbivores in turn rely on the leafy forests to survive."

"All right. So the dust cloud cuts off the photosynthesis of the forests, the herbivores starve . . ." Zeke sighed.

"And the lupoids die for lack of prey. Got it," Jackson finished. He grinned at Zeke. "How 'bout it, Prof? Do I pass the class?"

Chapter Four

Zeke was relieved when the lander docked with the *Ostrom* without further incident. In many ways this was home for Zeke.

The *Ostrom* had originally been outfitted as a survey and prospecting ship by its first owner, with extensive laboratories, exploration equipment, storage bays for fuel and mineral samples, and quarters to keep a good-sized crew in comfort. It had two landers, both capable of unassisted launch into low orbit from bodies of up to two gravities. At that time, it was the *Ogilvie T. MacPherson*, one of the earliest ships to be equipped with invariance overdrive. Its basic propulsion was antimatter drive, with fully automated, fail-safe life support and navigation control, and complete hibernation facilities for the crew.

After Zeke got the ship and renamed it for the Old Yale scholar John Ostrom, he had augmented its facilities considerably. Its extensive laboratories now included instruments for excavation and recovery of artifacts. The storage areas could preserve living samples and the editing facilities allowed Sylvie to organize and polish the various records she took. The computer and complete library made the whole ship a mobile research and living center, all powered by BEC's unique invariance overdrive.

"We ought to be okay now," he said briefly, as he waited for the airlock to cycle.

"Yeah," said Jackson. "I think I'd welcome some joker taking us on, now that we have the full range of our facilities." He grinned at the thought.

"If we have to fight, we can fight." Zeke opened the airlock door and stepped through. A few moments later, they joined Kadak!xa on the bridge.

Sylvie laughed. "Should I record all this tough talk for posterity?" she asked.

"Welcome aboard, Zeke," said Kadak!xa. "Jackson, Sylvie."

Their !xaka! colleague looked like most of her species, two meters in length and standing about half a meter above the floor. Her segmented form arched backward so that her crustaceanlike head was upright. Her gills varied from brilliant purple to pale blue and her fourth segment was equipped with spinnerets. Spines extended from her carapace.

Now she was turning from the pilot's console to greet them. Lights from the readouts reflected on her gleaming bronze skin and the jangling metallic jewelry she wore that Zeke always found so garish.

"Hello, Kadak!xa!" Zeke said brightly. "You keep the chair for the time being."

"The console, you mean."

"My mistake, as usual." Zeke winked at her. She could not have fit in the standard human pilot's seat if she had wanted to.

She nodded slightly, bobbing the huge carapace along the top of her head.

"Shall we break orbit for Thomsen 4?" she asked.

"No. I want to have everyone briefed before we do anything else, especially me. And keep the alert going," added Zeke. "We were approached again on the way up here."

"Figures," growled Marty, behind him.

Zeke turned and grinned at the short, blocky architect. "No harm done, Marty."

"Yeah, I'll bet." His rocklike, chiseled features frowned. As a native of Tau Ceti 4, he had a face that seemed like a cross between a human and a turtle. That appearance belied a brain that housed a superb gift for divining the function of a structure from a few remaining archaeological scraps. "What did they do?"

"Turned tail," said Jackson. "As soon as we showed a real interest in them."

"Kadak!xa, do you have any more on the Thomsen 4 situation?" Zeke asked.

"Yes, I do. Ready for it?"

"Almost," Zeke said, turning to Jackson and Sylvie. "Five minutes to change and clean up. Then I want to convene right here for a full discussion."

The other two nodded and retired to quarters. Zeke started after them, wincing as he worked his sore shoulder.

"Hey, Zeke." Marty's expression turned to one of concern. "You go and hurt yourself? What really happened down there? Let me look." With a gentleness surprising in his thick, stubby fingers, he pulled back Zeke's uniform.

"It's just bruising."

"Yeah . . . well, all right. You'll live." Marty shook his head. "I don't know how, considering the way you run your life."

Zeke laughed and went to clean up.

Washing up quickly and changing into another outfit only took a moment. He collapsed on a reclining lounger in his quarters with a deep breath, knowing that even a moment alone could help him compose his thoughts. Prof. Ezekiel Bones, instructor, had been left behind already. Now Dr. Bones, field archaeologist, anthropologist, and self-appointed savior, was about to depart on another field trip. Sometimes a moment of solitude helped him re-orient his priorities.

This time he did not bother to mull over the mystery of the sniper, for which he knew he did not have enough clues. Instead, he simply closed his eyes and rested.

Several moments later, feeling a touch refreshed, he bounded out of his quarters and returned to the bridge.

The entire crew was settled on the bridge, with Sylvie recording. Kadak!xa turned over the ship to computer control and called up her file on Thomsen 4. Before Zeke could say anything, Marty jumped right in with a gruff demand.

"What's all the excitement about, anyhow?" Marty growled.

"What do you mean?" Zeke asked.

"Somebody has already made plans to divert the comet, haven't they? So what business do we have with Thomsen 4? Or have you all been misleading me again?" He looked around at the group.

"You're right, Marty," said Zeke. "As far as we know, someone does have plans to divert the comet. Kadak!xa, have you identified who this anonymous person is?"

"Yes," said Kadak!xa. "The developer is a woman named Corlissa Murdock. Have you met her?"

"I've heard of her," said Zeke. "What do you know about her?"

"She has a good record of business with Bones Energy Corporation," said Kadak!xa.

"BEC does business all over known space." Zeke shrugged.

"She even had BEC outfit her ship with invariance overdrive," Kadak!xa went on.

"Wait a minute," said Jackson, uncrossing his booted ankles. "You say a *good* record of business?"

"As far as we know."

"The record is extensive," said Sylvie, nodding her agreement.

"Then why is she having people shoot at us? And follow us around in space?" Jackson looked at Zeke. "You sure you've never met her—and gotten on her bad side somehow?"

"Not that I recall." Zeke shrugged again. "We don't have enough to go on to make a guess."

"Maybe it's not her," said Sylvie.

"So far, she's the only other person involved with Thomsen 4 we know about," said Jackson. "I'm not trying to jump to conclusions. But until we have another candidate, we'd better find out all we can about her."

"I've only spoken with one of her assistants," said Kadak!xa. "Their plan is to divert a small planetoid on the outer reaches of the Thomsen star system so that it collides with the comet."

"Do they have one in sight?" Marty asked, shaking his head. "It's a fine plan, but they better have the right rock in the right place at the right time."

Kadak!xa consulted her screen again. "Apparently they estimate that more than one planetoid will come into the proper area of space in time to do this. Asteroids, maybe. It doesn't say."

"She'd better have a lot of energy at her disposal," said Jackson. "Diverting a comet by hitting it with a planetoid may take a sizeable planetoid."

"True," said Zeke. "And knocking the planetoid out of its existing orbit into the comet will require a lot of energy from somewhere."

"That's about all we know about her plans," said Kadak!xa. "She has a salvage archaeologist named Calvin Louie on Thomsen 4 who's been there for some years now, since her first surveying expedition. That was the trip they turned up the collision course with the big comet. She left this Calvin Louie behind to make friends with the Arrs and catalogue the place."

"That's why I was checking the gallery," said Jackson. "He's in a position to loot if he wants to. How would anybody know until it's too late?"

"I know something about that," said Zeke. "I read about a presentation she made. She came back to Earth and reported the coming collision with the comet. That's how I knew about it in the first place."

"Right. As to the further details of her plans, her assistant got rather coy."

"Hmm. The farther away from Thomsen 4 she knocks something into the comet," said Zeke, "the less impact she'll need."

"They better do it soon," said Jackson. "If they hit it far enough away from Thomsen 4, a slight nudge will turn into a major directional shift by the time the comet nears Thomsen 4."

"Murdock, Inc., figures they can make the comet miss by a safe margin," said Kadak!xa.

"Ha! How sure can they be?" Marty shook his head.

"They're so sure that they're making plans to establish a colony on Thomsen 4 after the danger has passed."

"Yeah, yeah." Marty nodded cynically. "So that's why we're really going, eh?"

"You know me." Zeke lifted his hands as if in surrender. "The lupoid culture is going to be disrupted to some extent by any development of the planet . . ."

"And you want to put a word in for their well-being." Marty finished. "It sounds good to me, no matter how reputable a developer she is."

"I'm also thinking of the artifacts of their earliest cultural development," said Zeke. "I don't want those bulldozed. Sylvie, you said there was some controversy over the status of the lupoids—these Arrs."

"They give it a very guttural pronunciation. Nearly a growl."

"I can say that. *Arrrr*." Marty growled.

They all laughed.

"Let's make all our jokes here in private," said Zeke. "That's all I ask, okay?"

Marty nodded, as Zeke knew he would.

"Now, then," Zeke continued. "If a question exists as to the sentience of the Arrs, then we'll want proof that they qualify as an intelligent species. Without it, we won't be able to protect them as well from outside interference."

"The controversy definitely exists," said Sylvie. "According to the records I've reviewed, they use some basic tools and weapons and have at least a rudimentary vocabulary. That much is agreed upon."

"So to ice the argument, we'll want some examples of art, especially if it's related to a religion," said Zeke.

"Or sophisticated tools and weapons," said Jackson. "That will help, if they're complex enough."

"I can verify the levels of intelligence required for certain architectural designs if we're lucky enough to find the right evidence," said Marty. "Variety is the main thing.Creatures that build by instinct always build along the same basic concept. Intelligent species keep improving, modifying. But they may not be at the building stage yet."

"We don't know if their vocabulary qualifies as a language or just a list of symbols," said Sylvie. "That will help, too."

"As usual," said Zeke, "everything is tied together. If we can communicate with them amicably, we can find the rest of our answers."

"And if not," said Sylvie, "we'll just make all the observations we can."

"Exactly," said Zeke.

"Like you were saying earlier, Zeke," said Sylvie. "It's the billiard ball effect again. You influence one item, then it strikes on the next, and so on."

"Why aren't we on our way to Thomsen 4?" Marty demanded. "Why are we just sitting here?"

"On Earth I was anxious to get on our way," said Zeke. "But now I want opinions from everyone. Can anybody think of any clues to our attackers?" He looked around.

"I still don't see why we can't talk on the way," said Marty.

"Since the attacks have been on or near Earth, it's just possible that whoever or whatever is behind it is here."

Jackson shook his head, staring at the floor in front of him. "I've been thinking about this ever since we took off, and I can't think of anything. We've just been ambushed by a stranger."

"I ordered the computer to correlate all information that might lead to an answer," said Kadak!xa. "It doesn't come to anything."

"You got me," Marty said bluntly.

"All right, gang," Zeke said decisively. "Enough talk for now. Prepare for hibernation. We're off for Thomsen 4 immediately, on I.O."

"*Now* you're talking!" Jackson pounded his fist in exuberance and grinned as he stood up.

"'Bout time," Marty muttered to himself, rising also.

The entire group started out, still talking.

"Maybe the attack by the art gallery was also a diversion," said Sylvie. "One that the sniper botched by not running away and by getting himself killed instead."

"There is still more to this than I can understand," said Zeke. "I just don't feel Murdock is behind this."

"We don't have any hard evidence either way," Kadak!xa reminded him, turning her great ridged face slightly to face him.

Zeke nodded his acknowledgement. "That's based on gut feeling only, but . . . does anyone else feel different?"

Jackson shrugged.

"She has no history to suggest these tactics," said Kadak!xa. "Pardon me for repeating myself."

"And she may not even know of your interest in the Thomsen 4 situation," Sylvie added.

"Or care, if she does know," Zeke finished. "I'm not against development of the planet and I'm certainly in favor of her diverting the comet. So what's going on?"

"Maybe," Marty said slowly, "she's planning to do something on the planet that she knows you won't like when you find out about it. How about that?"

Zeke shook his head. "That's as good a guess as any."

They all began to get ready for hibernation.

The entire team was experienced at invariance overdrive aboard the *Ostrom*. It was a rare and highly expensive piece of technology, but the concept was simple enough. The ship would aim for the current location of Thomsen 4, or more precisely as close in space as it could get safely. With the crew in hibernation, it would travel in normal time to that spot. By the time it arrived, of course, the planet would have moved to another point in space. However, the *Ostrom* would then jump backward in time to the moment of departure, when Thomsen 4 was still near the point in space where the *Ostrom* appeared.

Chapter Five

Zeke climbed into his hibernation chamber satisfied that the answers to the mysteries plaguing them would be found on Thomsen 4. A mild painkiller had eased the discomfort in his shoulder. He shut off all lights and quickly went to sleep in the darkness after the activities and stresses of the day.

A faint beeping sound near his head brought him out of sleep. A yellow light was blinking, throwing its color into the darkness around him. That was an emergency alert—he had been automatically brought out of hibernation by computer. He wondered where they were—and when they were.

Now his adrenalin began to flow from a long-established habit. He drew in a deep breath to increase the oxygen flow to his forebrain.

"Unknown ship approaching," said the voice of the computer. "Yellow alert still operable."

"Go to red alert," Zeke snapped at the wall mike. "Where are we?"

"In orbit around Thomsen 4 in the Thomsen star system."

"What? Why weren't we awakened already? How long have we been here?"

"The *Ostrom* has been in the Thomsen star system approximately fifty-one seconds."

Zeke swung his legs out of the bunk and pulled his suit on as the red alert siren began to wail throughout the *Ostrom*. At least they had arrived. Apparently someone had been waiting for them.

Jackson was in the pilot's chair by the time Zeke reached the bridge. Under red alert, that duty went to whoever got there first. Sylvie was on the communicator.

"Any i.d. on the ship yet?" Zeke asked. He remained in the middle of the bridge.

"No," said Sylvie. "I'm hailing, to no response as usual." She nodded toward the viewscreen, where a point of light against a grid represented the other ship.

"Where are we?" Zeke asked Jackson. "The computer said that ship was approaching us."

"That was the first assessment," said Jackson. "Now the computer says we're on converging courses ahead."

"And where are we to converge, as far as we can tell?"

"On the far side of Thomsen 4."

Zeke nodded.

"Delightful," Marty said irritably, as he plodded in, trailing one hand on the wall.

"Still no answer, eh?" Zeke asked, studying the tiny mark on the viewscreen.

"No," said Sylvie.

"Jackson, let's go after them."

Jackson grinned. "You got it." He entered the order.

Kadak!xa joined Zeke near the middle of the bridge. Together, they watched the viewscreen as the unidentified ship altered its course to approach the *Ostrom*, even as they were chasing it.

"Projectiles coming," she called gruffly.

"Oh, wonderful," muttered Marty.

Jackson ordered defensive laser fire. According to the readout under his viewscreen, the computer had identified the missiles as standard, non-nuclear heat seekers. The *Ostrom* should be able to detonate them easily.

"Defensive fire underway," he informed the others.

Around him, the others took their places on the bridge. By the time Zeke looked at the viewscreen again, the brightly colored explosions were already signifying that the lasers had set off the missiles at a safe distance.

"More projectiles coming; more laser fire going." Jackson also ordered the computer to fire back at the enemy ship with similar projectile weapons.

So far, Zeke didn't really feel the *Ostrom* was in danger.

As Zeke continued to watch the screen, bright flashes appeared from the laser weapons of the other ship.

"This is insane," said Jackson. "They're firing lasers at us."

He was right, Zeke thought. The *Ostrom*'s shiny surface should have told the enemy that it would reflect their laser beams easily.

"Don't they have any idea of what they're doing?" Jackson wondered aloud.

"Guess not," said Marty. "Are we being attacked by morons, or what?" He looked over at Zeke. "Have you made any stupid people mad lately, Ezekiel?"

"I'm starting to think so," said Zeke thoughtfully.

As expected, the lasers were reflecting harmlessly off the surface of the *Ostrom*.

"Sylvie, try hailing them," said Zeke. "See if they'll talk."

"Now hailing," said Sylvie.

"I wouldn't give them a breather," said Jackson.

"Good point. Just disable them if you can. We'll try pinpoint aim with projectiles, accompanied by particle beams, aiming for their weapons. Live prisoners will tell us more than dead ones."

"You got it," said Jackson. He released a scattered pattern of missiles laced with particle beams. The lasers were occupied defensively, where they were the most useful.

Both ships were taking evasive moves as they fired at each other. The enemy ship successfully dodged all the *Ostrom*'s fire at first, but the *Ostrom*'s computer analyzed the enemy's pattern of movement and incorporated it into its pattern of fire as it continued to shoot.

"Sylvie?" Zeke called.

"No response," she answered.

Finally one of the *Ostrom*'s particle beams caught the enemy's missile launcher.

"Let's head right for them!" Jackson shouted. "Come on, Zeke! Let's go after them."

"Agreed," Kadak!xa rumbled ominously.

Zeke glanced over at her. She had been remarkably calm and businesslike while the welfare of the *Ostrom* had been her responsibility. Now some of the temper of her species were starting to show.

"All right. Let's see what they do."

Jackson took the manual controls himself and drove straight for the enemy ship, while the computer continued to fire at it.

The enemy ship swung about and fled.

Jackson followed, maintaining speed. He stopped firing.

Suddenly the enemy ship whipped about on a short turning radius, dropped beneath the range of the viewscreen, and headed another way.

"Forget this," Zeke said suddenly. "They're just playing with us, whoever they are."

"What do you mean?" Kadak!xa asked.

"I think they want to draw us off," said Zeke. "Maybe this whole operation was another diversion."

Both ships were still firing at each other. The enemy ship used its lasers to explode the *Ostrom*'s projectiles, the same way the *Ostrom* was eliminating the enemy missiles. However, behind those silent explosions, the other ship again changed course abruptly and fled.

Jackson gave chase.

"No," Zeke said firmly. "On to Thomsen 4."

"You sure?" Jackson asked, but he was already altering the ship's course.

"Definitely," said Zeke. "This attack looked even more like a diversion than the last one. Maybe all of them were, like Sylvie said earlier."

"Somebody doesn't want us on Thomsen 4," Marty agreed. "And I, for one, am getting tired of being the only target in a shooting gallery no one told us about."

Now that the excitement was over for the moment, they all had a chance to compose themselves. Jackson remained in the pilot's chair under the yellow alert while the others went to shower and eat. It certainly was not the first time this group had had its routine disrupted on a Dr. Bones project.

When Zeke and the others returned to the bridge, Thomsen 4 hung large and greenish blue in the sky.

"Sylvie, what can we expect down there?" Zeke asked.

She paused to consult her records. "The Arrs we have data on live in a heavily forested, slightly rolling terrain. The zone is temperate and right now the temperatures are dry and mild, though thunderstorms can come up quickly."

Jackson raised his eyebrows. "That sounds great. Almost too comfortable to believe."

"It fits," said Sylvie. "Lupoids as a group often develop in lush forests."

"It sounds like the place that art gallery of yours was in," said Zeke. "Except that was mountains." He looked at the screen again.

"It even resembles Earth," said Sylvie.

"Don't keep us in suspense, boss man," said Marty gruffly. "Who's going down there into the unknown and who's staying home to wait for the next turkey shoot?"

"Sylvie, Marty, and Jackson will come down with me. Kadak!xa, maintain yellow alert and once we're there, take ongoing evasive orbital moves." He took them all in at a glance. "All right, gang, let's get ready. By the time we're prepared, we'll be in orbit. We'll take the unwinged lander."

When the landing team was ready and the *Ostrom* in position, Zeke piloted the lander down into the atmosphere of Thomsen 4. They were aiming for a heavily forested area where much of the data on the Arrs had been gathered at an earlier time.

Several different Arr communities had been noted in the region at that time. The earlier studies had gathered so little information, however, that Sylvie couldn't guarantee the Arrs would still be there. Even so, Zeke felt it was the place to start.

"Sylvie, are you sure we can land this thing in the right area?" Zeke asked. "We don't need much open space, but we do need some."

"The last two excursions to Thomsen 4 came down in that spot in similar landers of about the same size," said Sylvie. "My records are clear on that question."

"Okay," said Zeke, shrugging.

On their first low-altitude pass, Zeke found that a number of clear areas dotted what was otherwise heavy forest. The clearings were often on the crest of low rises—not mountains, certainly, but small ridges and mounds. They were foothills of a real mountain range that was part of the region Arrs were known to have inhabited. The mountains were visible and also heavily forested.

"Are those burn areas?" Jackson wondered, studying the bare ridges below.

"Doesn't look like it to me," said Marty.

"I'll check," said Sylvie. She consulted some of her records through an earring that doubled as an earphone. "Mmm—no. Apparently they represent some tilted rock layers that have a different composition from the surface layers of the level forest. The trees just won't grow on some of them."

"Good enough," said Zeke. "Here we go."

This unwinged lander was able to descend vertically onto the rounded crest of a mound. The mound rose roughly fifteen meters from the surrounding land. It was covered with two-meter high green grasses and surrounded on all sides by dense forest.

"I'm taking recordings on all sides," said Sylvie.

"Good," said Zeke. "Sylvie, can you calculate any odds that we're near an Arr community here?"

"No." Sylvie shook her head emphatically, sending her hair and jewelry swaying. "We aren't sure how many or which ones are nomadic. We might have to look a long time or we could be right next to a large community."

"All right," said Zeke. "Remember, gang, we expect them to be friendly."

"Famous last words," Marty muttered.

Zeke ignored him. "Stay alert, though, because they aren't used to strangers. Everyone ready?" He looked around.

Jackson nodded.

"Let's go."

Zeke opened the door and Jackson stepped out first, holding his laser rifle ready. Zeke followed him out, also alert for trouble. Marty and Sylvie remained inside but ready to follow.

High grasses waved all around them. The green forest at the base of the mound was silent. The same breeze that swept the grasses also brushed the leaves of the trees.

"All clear," Jackson reported, looking around. "Poor visibility in the forest, though. No more than four meters, I'd say."

Zeke looked, shading the sunlight with one hand over his eyes. The high grasses made walking difficult. He made room for Marty and Sylvie, who stepped out behind him.

The trees of the forest rose up many meters, but in the distance Zeke could see a cliff that rose even higher."

Sylvie pointed to it. "I recommend moving that way."

"Why?" Zeke asked.

"One researcher was sure that a large Arr community had staked out its territory in a radius around the cliff," said Sylvie. "He guessed that they lived at least partly in caves here, but he wasn't able to get there to prove it."

"Are we in that radius now?"

"Yes, easily."

"All right. We'll head that way." Zeke nodded. "I'll walk point. Sylvie, you stay behind me to keep us on course. Then Marty, and Jackson in the rear."

Zeke began to wade through the grasses down the slope. He was watching his footing when Marty yelled, "Zeke!"

At the same time, Jackson shouted, "Incoming!"

Zeke whipped out one of his hand lasers and looked up. Four spears—no, they were gigantic arrows—were flying out of the forest at them, spaced perhaps six meters apart but converging fast.

"Fire high! Don't hit any Arrs!" Zeke yelled as he slid down into the grass.

Jackson's laser fire raked the leaves of the trees at the base of the mound, at a height above the unseen Arrs. Zeke also fired his hand laser at a similar height, hoping to deter them without hurting them. One of the hugh arrows, easily the size of an ancient human spear, stuck in the ground two meters up the slope from where he lay.

Then he saw some Arrs for the first time. They stepped up into the spaces between the trees at the edge of the forest, some of them holding spears, slings, and hand weapons. He could not see the source of the big arrows.

They were perhaps a meter and a half tall, walking upright but a little stooped. Their hind legs had hocks, not knees, and their substantial haunches implied considerable jumping ability. They had wolflike faces with short snouts and erect pointed ears set on the sides of their heads, in a near-human position.

"Sylvie! Can you speak to them?" He called out, ducking down into the grasses to where he was unable to see anything but the grass.

"I can try," she called back, from her own hiding place elsewhere in the grass. "The vocabulary I have for them is only one researcher's opinion. We don't know if it's really a language or not."

A throwing stick and a rock landed hard near Zeke.

"Try it!"

She began a series of guttural shouts.

The Arrs responded by heaving a volley of spears and stones and throwing sticks.

"Pull back!" Zeke shouted, rising up to fire again. This time he took careful aim and burned a hole in a tree trunk between a couple of Arrs. They started, looking at the smoking hole.

Zeke began sliding backward up the slope through the grass partly propped up on one arm so he could keep an eye on the Arrs.

"Sylvie!" Jackson shouted, from somewhere else in the grass. "Are you sure you aren't insulting them?"

"I'm calling 'friend' and that sort of thing," she called back. "Maybe it's the wrong dialect or something."

"Into the lander! Hurry!" Zeke paused to set afire some of the grass in front of the ARRS with a laser streak.

He saw for the first time, then, how those big arrows were launched. A little to his right on the edge of the forest, a very large Arr was lying on his back with his hind feet braced against a bow that must have been two meters long. He held it horizontally, pushed against tree trunks on either side to steady it, and pulled back on the string with both hands—Zeke could see the opposable thumbs for the first time, though their choice and style of weapons had implied thumbs already.

Zeke dodged a spear, keeping an eye on the big arrow. When it was launched toward him, he was just able to throw himself to one side in time to avoid it.

"Come on, Zeke!" Marty yelled. "You're the last one out. We're ready to launch!"

"Covering you," Jackson called calmly.

At that, Zeke jumped up and ran for the lander, plodding clumsily uphill through the high grasses. Now he could see Jackson standing at the entrance to the lander, firing his laser rifle back and forth in broad strokes. He fired either over the Arrs or into the ground just in front of him, by the angle of the gun.

Zeke slid into the lander behind him and found Sylvie in the pilot's chair. Jackson ducked inside and closed the entry. As the lander rose from the mound, they could hear the clunk and clatter of stones, sticks, and probably a big arrow or two against the hull.

Then, before any damage could be done, they had reached an altitude safe from the Arrs' weapons.

"Where to, Zeke?" Sylvie asked.

"Find another landing site," he said grimly, brushing hair out of his eyes.

"You sure?" she asked.

"Another mound or ridge, maybe higher than that last one. We'll be more careful next time."

"Wonderful," Marty muttered sourly.

"Anyone hurt?" Zeke looked around.

"No," said Jackson. "But someone is going to be if we don't get a better plan of action."

"Sylvie," said Zeke. "Do you have any idea why they gave us that reception?"

"No," said Sylvie. "Sorry, but I don't. They don't have any history to explain it."

"How about why they ignored your call of friendship?" Jackson asked. "Do you think they understood you at all?"

"I can't tell. I really have no idea. They may not have understood what I was saying. On the other hand, they may have just been too angry to care."

"I'm getting real tired of these mysterious attacks on our persons," said Marty. "It's happening every time we turn around, it seems." He shook his large head.

"You're not the only one, believe me." Zeke thought a moment. "Get Kadak!xa on the loudspeaker."

Sylvie had her a moment later.

"Give us a heat scan of this area," said Zeke. "Something has roused the Arrs in this area. I'm guessing that another ship has landed and stirred up trouble."

"Understood," said Kadak!xa. "I'm initiating a scan. I'll call back if I get anything."

"I have some possible landing sites," said Sylvie. "Shall we descend or wait for her scan?"

"We'll wait," said Zeke. "We can't afford another fight where they're trying to kill us and we won't hurt them."

"I've got something," said Kadak!xa, still on the speaker. "A concentrated heat source about a kilometer from you. No open flame is visible and this is not a volcanic area."

"That's it," said Zeke. "It means a level of technology far beyond the Arrs' capability. Sylvie, get the coordinates and land as close to it as you can."

Chapter Six

At first glance the next landing site looked identical to the last. It was a mound of about the same size lying considerably closer to the cliffs. A quick pass over the heat source showed it to be, as Zeke had guessed, a lander larger than their own but otherwise similar.

Not much else could be detected about it from the air. They were landing as close to it as they safely could. From there, they would have to go overland.

This time when Zeke and Jackson stepped out of the lander they immediately swept the surrounding forest area with laser fire, too high to hit any hidden Arrs. Then they waited. When they received no response, they did it again. Finally Zeke took a deep breath and exchanged a glance with Jackson.

"I don't think they're here," he said. "Of course I realize that doesn't mean we won't run headlong into them two minutes after we enter the forest."

"You know, Zeke . . ." said Jackson, lowering his laser rifle, "normally I don't argue with your values. In fact, ordinarily I might even be hotter to defend the natives of this planet than you are. But . . ."

"What?" Zeke looked up at him.

"What's the point of not shooting a few of them, if we can't save their entire species from being wiped out when the comet hits?" Jackson turned away to squint toward the forest ahead of them. "I don't mean we should attack them. But maybe we should defend ourselves well enough so we can move forward and do what we have to do."

Marty and Sylvie had come out behind them, ready to go. Sylvie closed the lander entry. "All clear, huh?"

"The idea of killing a few people in a group to save the rest from themselves is a very old imperialist argument," said Zeke. "It offends me a lot."

"All we have to do is defend ourselves," said Marty. "That ought to be our operating principle."

"Fair enough," said Jackson. "I don't really want to hurt them, either, you know."

"If we hurt any of them, we'll lose their cooperation for sure," said Zeke. "That won't help us save them."

"Maybe if Kadak!xa came down," said Sylvie. "Her size and appearance might intimidate the Arrs and open up the way for us without hurting any of them."

"We'd have to wait for her . . . and send someone up to take her place on the *Ostrom*. I don't want to leave it empty." Zeke shook his head. "I don't want any more delay, either."

"And it might not work," added Marty. "They aren't exactly timid. After all, they didn't hesitate to attack us."

"Let's go," said Zeke.

Zeke led the way down through the grasses into the forest, moving slowly and cautiously. He figured there was a good chance that the crew of the other lander had observed their presence. They were quite likely an enemy of some sort and the longer he took to move on them gave them more time to prepare a reception.

He had gone no more than ten meters into the forest, stepping over fallen branches and between large tree trunks, when he felt an overwhelming sense of vulnerability. The immense trees shut out almost all the light. What little filtered all the way through to the ground was indirect and diffuse.

The Arrs lived here and knew their way around. Zeke and his crew had very limited visibility and no familiarity with the terrain. He began to realize that if they were attacked by Arrs here, they might very well have to kill them, or be killed themselves.

Then a movement off to his left caught his eye, and he froze in position.

"Zeke," Sylvie said quietly. "My recording devices are picking up movement on all sides of us. Also straight ahead, backing away as we advance."

"Arrs?"

"All I have is sound and a couple of partial appearances, but I would say so. It's always possible that we've attracted a pack of predators, though."

Zeke smiled faintly. "Well, those we can shoot if we have to. We aren't obligated to become anyone's dinner."

"Did you say dinner?" Marty demanded, in a louder voice from behind Sylvie.

"Easy, Marty," said Zeke, still looking around as he worked his way between a couple of large bushes. "We can talk, I think, but stay in line and don't do anything to surprise anyone."

"Company, eh?" Jackson said, from his position in the rear. "I thought I heard something."

"Let's just keep moving," said Zeke. "So far, they're just observing. Maybe we can keep it that way."

Their progress remained slow. It was a first-stage growth, of course, as primeval as one could find. If the Arrs had regular pathways through it, Zeke was not on one of them.

The group was constantly climging over fallen logs, or working its way between huge tree trunks growing close together. Several times the network of roots and small branches beneath their feet gave way into soft, moist soil, momentarily trapping them by the ankles. Jackson's weight, in particular, caused his boots to crash through ground cover of that sort. Zeke used his hand laser to cut away branches and roots when he had to, but he was reluctant to spend energy he might need later to defend them all.

Frequently he could not find a way around or through some of the tangles and obstacles'. Then he had to pick his way through a detour, trying to remain on course at the end of it. Sylvie's data helped them maintain their direction.

He was pushing his way through some thick, chest-high branches with both hands when Sylvie spoke.

"Zeke," she said, behind him.

"Yeah?"

"I have a line of our company's footsteps moving very smoothly now off to our left, almost parallel with our course. It might be a path we could use."

Zeke nodded and began slogging through the underbrush to his right. He was surprised that the ground cover was so thick in a forest where light was sparse, but apparently some of the short, lush, broad-leaved plants required no more light than this to flourish.

Suddenly Zeke stumbled out of the underbrush onto a narrow path. It was no wider than two human feet side by side, but it was a relief from the constant effort of battling the forest footing. Branches still crisscrossed the path.

"They know we've found the path," said Sylvie. "They're gathering ahead of us."

Zeke looked at the way the path wound ahead. It was clearly visible for only about six meters, but a small space in the tree trunks ahead implied its direction a little farther. He couldn't see any Arrs anywhere, though.

"It's heading generally toward that other lander," said Zeke. "We'll follow it if they let us."

Traveling on the path was much faster. At one point, however, Zeke ducked under a branch, came around a bend, and found a tall Arr standing squarely ahead of him, holding a spear upright. Zeke came to an abrupt halt.

The Arr made no move and no sound. He watched Zeke with bright, dark eyes.

"What is it—" Marty started, but someone, probably Jackson, silenced him.

"Sylvie," Zeke said, without looking away from the Arr. "See if you can speak to him."

Sylvie uttered another series of growling sounds. The Arr watched her without moving. Then he turned off the path and disappeared into the forest.

"That's a lot different from our last reception," said Zeke. "Their whole pattern of behavior is a change from that hostile welcome we received. Is this a different group?"

"I'm certain it is," said Sylvie. "I don't have any proof to give you, though."

Zeke proceeded with the group still following him in single file along the path. They had covered some distance when Sylvie spoke softly behind him again.

"They're gone," she said.

"Gone? Do you know where?" Zeke asked, still moving ahead. "Did they rush off or just wander away?"

"They just withdrew as a group and headed to our left. I don't think they were in a hurry, but we just don't know enough about their behavior to guess at the significance of their moves."

"What are they doing now?"

"I don't know." Sylvie shrugged. "I'm not picking up any vibrations now at all."

"Keep monitoring."

At last they reached the edge of the forest, where the mysterious stronghold rose up from another grass-covered hill. A lander made up most of it, but it possessed some added facilities. Every few seconds, brightly colored electrical flashes crackled through the air around it in a kind of fence.

"Marty?" Zeke said quietly. He was standing just inside the line of the forest, looking up at the sunlit lander. "From the design of the lander, its origin is human. What else?"

Marty came forward. He looked over the stronghold for a moment without speaking.

"That lander is a Hamilcar 9000," offered Jackson.

"All right, simple enough," Marty said gruffly. "That rig on the top is a compact solar converter. Those flashes come from it. Sylvie, give me your readouts on the energy usage. Ozone levels, anything."

Sylvie consulted her equipment for a moment. Then she quoted some numbers.

"Zeke, that fence isn't dangerous," said Marty. "It might sting. Basically, it's designed to scare away Arrs and animals, I would say."

"Is it dangerous at all?"

"Well, it wouldn't kill Arrs or us," said Marty. "Small animals, pests, yes."

"In that case, maybe the inhabitants aren't going to be unpleasant," said Zeke. "Sylvie, see if you can raise anyone."

"Now hailing," she said.

"You sure, Zeke?" Jackson asked. "They may be more concerned about Arrs than about us. After all, somebody's been shooting at us for some reason."

"We haven't shown ourselves yet. Sylvie, are you getting anything?" Zeke asked.

"Not yet. But if they have monitors set up, they know we're here by now."

"Just keep recording. We'll all take a circuit together around the perimeter of the clearing and get a look at this place from every angle." Zeke waved for them to follow.

The forest was a little sparser on the edge, so they were able to move through it without too much trouble. Zeke was encouraged by Marty's assessment of the fence as well, feeling that anyone careful not to harm the Arrs would at least be willing to negotiate before starting to shoot. Still, he kept inside the forest just in case.

By the time they had completed a full circuit of the stronghold, Sylvie had still not raised a response from within it.

"Something else is bothering me," Zeke said, as they stopped to gaze at the silent hill again. "Whoever designed this did not want to hurt any Arrs, and yet that first group was extremely hostile toward us. Since the first impression of us they had was our lander, I wonder if they associated us with this one. Could the owner of this place have created that much bad feeling?"

"That hostility was not recorded on Murdock's first trip here," said Sylvie. "It's new, at least since then."

"Call Kadak!xa," said Zeke. "Ask if she can detect any other heat sources or signs of technology above Arr level."

As Sylvie did so, Jackson stepped up next to Zeke. "What do you think? Shall we go and knock?"

"I think it's more likely that no one's home. The inhabitant, or inhabitants, are probably out pursuing their daily activities, whatever they are."

"And you don't want to snoop around uninvited."

Zeke punched him lightly on the arm with a grin. "You know better than that."

"Kadak!xa can't help much, I'm afraid," said Sylvie.

"Nothing, eh?" Zeke said.

"She has no further evidence of advanced technology and of course the forest obscures her line of sight, too."

"What about locating individuals by body heat?" Marty demanded. "If she's in the right position."

"Our heat sensors aren't much help because the Arrs are roughly the same size and body temperature as humans," said Sylvie. "She has detected plenty of life-forms the right size, but if there are people nearby besides us, she can't tell which ones are which."

"I shoulda known," muttered Marty.

"All right," said Zeke. "Either we force our way inside this place, which I refuse to do, or we go looking for its owner somewhere else. Sylvie, see if correlating any of your data can give us some tracks away from here that we can follow. I didn't see any by naked eye when we walked around the hill."

"Neither did I," said Jackson.

"I might have something," said Sylvie. "It's not a set of tracks, though, and it's faint."

"What is it?"

"The forest ground cover is just a little thinner in a narrow line, starting over there." She pointed along the edge of the forest to a spot not too far away. "It might be a path beaten by infrequent footsteps or it might be a coincidence."

"One way to find out," said Zeke. "Lead the way."

When Sylvie had reached the area in question, Zeke found the ground to have more rocks in it than most of the forest floor.

"That doesn't mean it's not a path," he pointed out. "Maybe our quarry started walking here because of the rocks. It's more solid and fewer branches get in the way. I'll lead from here. Stay alert, everybody. Sylvie, keep an ear out for footsteps of any kind."

A short distance later, when the rocky ground gave out, the line was clearly a path. It even had a few footprints in it here and there. Zeke stopped to consider them.

"I know you, Zeke," said Jackson. "You're getting some ideas. How about it?"

"So far it looks like only one person," Zeke said slowly. "Don't you think?"

"Agreed," said Jackson, with a shrug.

"I'm starting to think that this person is raiding Arr belongings. That's why no one is home at the moment, back on the hill. It also would explain the Arr hostility and wariness, even if they aren't actually being killed."

Jackson nodded. "I'll buy that. If he's alone, though, he must be using superior weapons to pull this off."

"Say, look up," said Marty in surprise. "Is that where we're headed, do you think?"

Zeke looked up. Through the very tops of the trees, some rocky bluffs were just barely visible between the leafy branches.

"They aren't too far," Jackson observed.

"I'll bet that's our destination," said Zeke. "At a glance those bluffs look like they just might be full of limestone caves. A large community of Arrs could reside there."

"Maybe enough for two separate groups," said Marty. "Two tribes, or whatever they use. That would explain why we've received two different receptions."

"Is that likely?" Zeke asked. "Two tribes this close together?"

Marty shrugged. "We might have landed on the border between their territories or in the middle of a civil war in one tribe. Or maybe one lives in the forest and the other on the bluffs. It's possible."

As they proceeded, the path remained faint and narrow for a long time. Zeke looked up every so often and found that they were definitely heading right toward the bluffs. They were rounded, though steep, at the base. He expected to find paths leading upward when he reached them. Sylvie continued monitoring her sensors but reported no sign of unseen companions.

The cliffs loomed just overhead when Zeke noticed something new on the trail. He stopped, studying the faint imprints in the soft ground cover at his feet.

"Zeke?" Jackson said quietly. "What is it?"

"Our friend was joined by some company."

"ARRS, you mean," said Marty.

"Almost certainly."

"I'm getting major vibrations," said Sylvie. "Sound should be audible to the naked ear, at least faintly." She pointed up at the high cliffs. "Up there somewhere."

"A whining sound," said Zeke. "A power tool?"

"That's what I think." Sylvie nodded.

Zeke set his jaw angrily. "Cutting away artifacts, no doubt."

Sylvie nodded again.

"So we have a raider of some kind to deal with," Zeke said. "All right. Let's go."

The merged footsteps followed the path through the forest. As the ground began to rise, the forest became thinner until it finally fell away completely. They were picking their footing carefully among rocks, high grasses, and occasional bushes as the path gradually wound its way up the slope.

Eventually the path grew steeper and became a thin line of steps angling up the lower portion of the cliff face. The mouth of a large cave was in sight ahead, the opening perhaps four meters high and five wide. The whining sound was now clearly emanating from it, probably that of a saw cutting rock.

Zeke drew his hand weapon and looked back at the others. Jackson had moved into position right behind him. Marty followed, with Sylvie in the rear where she could record all the events that would unfold in front of her.

Jackson nodded readiness. Zeke crouched low and stepped quietly forward, around the edge of the cave mouth. The scene in front of him was almost exactly what he expected.

Chapter Seven

A human stood to the right side of the cave. He might have been Zeke's age or a little younger, of Asian descent. The only human here, he was apparently supervising a small group of Arrs.

The man was watching a large Arr use a hand-sized rock saw against the left wall of the cave. The Arr was perhaps nine meters in from the cave mouth, illuminated by the bright sunlight slanting into the cave mouth.

The Arr was holding the saw steady as it bit into the cave wall and sent a fine powder spinning out onto the cave floor. The whining sound was high-pitched and loud. From the Arr's facility with the saw, Zeke judged that he had had considerable experience in cutting out rock artifacts.

In the same moment that Zeke took that scene in, he also registered the existence of paintings and relief carvings on the wall. The Arr was apparently cutting them out. Even more immediate, however, was the presence of four more Arrs all turning toward Zeke.

Two of them held Arr spears. The other two held hand lasers similar to the one in Zeke's hand. All four stiffened in surprise and began to raise their weapons.

The man inside the cave had also turned to look. He shouted something unintelligible and the Arrs stopped moving. The one with the rock saw shut it off.

"That was a wise move," said Zeke, who had already been holding his laser aimed directly at the man. "Who are you?"

Jackson stepped up alongside him, holding his laser rifle on one of the Arrs with a laser weapon.

"I might ask you the same," said the man in the cave. He nodded toward the Arrs. "I ordered them to keep their weapons low. Yours aren't necessary."

"Jackson, Marty," said Zeke.

Jackson and Marty stepped forward and collected the laser weapons and spears from the Arrs. Marty kept the lasers and Jackson tossed the spears out of the cave. Then they returned to Zeke's side.

"I'm Dr. Ezekiel Bones," said Zeke coldly. "And I'm getting impatient. Who are you, why are you here . . . and why are you stealing and destroying the art and sacred icons of a living culture?"

To Zeke's surprise, the man seemed to relax slightly. "Dr. Bones! I'm glad to meet you. I'm Calvin Louie, salvage archaeologist. I've been surveying and recording data for Corlissa Murdock."

Zeke lowered his weapon and spoke over his shoulder without taking his eyes off Calvin. "Sylvie?"

Sylvie was standing behind them at the cave mouth. She hesitated, consulting her records. "That's the name of her salvage archaeologist, all right. But I don't have a picture."

"You call this wanton destruction salvage?" Zeke demanded, waving a hand at the cave wall. Now that he looked, he also saw large sealed containers stacked neatly against both walls. "I see you have plenty of items ready for export at a hefty profit."

"That's not true at all," Calvin retorted heatedly. "This culture has a very short lifetime left, Dr. Bones. A large comet is due to strike this planet in a matter of weeks. Anything made of this limestone that I don't get off the surface is going to crack apart in the extreme cold of the cometary winter to follow anyway. The Arrs are certain to become extinct, unless you have a ship big enough to move them all . . . because I certainly don't."

"Nice try, Dr. Louie . . . if that's who you are." Zeke shook his head. "It just so happens that I know that Corlissa Murdock is going to divert the comet."

"That would make a handy double cross," said Jackson grimly. "He takes everything off the planet under a reasonable excuse, and by the time the planet is saved he's sold it all who-knows-where."

"Hold it!" Calvin shouted, pointing at both of them. "Haven't you heard? Corlissa's business is in trouble and she can't afford to divert the comet any more."

Zeke stared at him. "What? No, we hadn't . . . Just how recent is that development?"

Calvin looked pointedly at the laser weapon Zeke still held, though it was now aimed downward.

Zeke stuck it in the back of his belt, secure in the knowledge that the Arrs had been disarmed and that Jackson was still scowling over his laser rifle at the lot of them.

"Corlissa came back here less than a week ago," said Calvin. "She's in orbit upstairs right now."

"Doing what?" Jackson demanded.

"Making as much space as possible for cargo." Calvin nodded to the stacks of sealed containers. "She's to come back to take me off the planet and everything I can salvage at the same time."

"I'll have to double-check your—"

"Zeke," Sylvie said sharply. "Company coming."

"Eh? What do you mean?"

"Vibrations down below." Sylvie stepped forward. "Perhaps ten or twenty Arrs, moving this way in a body. The forest cover blocks all sight of them so far."

"I'd retrieve those spears you tossed out of the cave," said Calvin grimly.

"They're coming on quickly," said Sylvie. She turned and looked out the mouth of the cave. "I think they're gathering at the edge of the forest, just before the bluff turns to rock and grass."

"Are they with you?" Zeke demanded, turning to Calvin.

"No," said Calvin. "The reason I armed the four Arrs with me here is that you're right—we're taking art and sacred symbols from the Arrs. These four are renegades, really . . ."

"And the bulk of the locals aren't too happy about the whole operation," Zeke finished. "I wish I could take your word for that, no insult intended."

Calvin shrugged, but he gave Zeke a look of impatient disgust.

Sylvie moved aside and concentrated on her equipment.

Marty took a couple of wary glances down the bluff. The Arrs were not in sight yet. He then carefully eased down the terrace of the cave to get the spears. His short, bulky form had a low center of gravity that helped him maneuver on the slope. The spears were not far, but reaching them was awkward. The others watched as he hurried back up to the cave gripping a spear in each hand.

"Keep them," Zeke said. "Calvin, you and your companions stand against the far wall there."

"They aren't going to make conversation, Dr. Bones," said Calvin. "They're going to attack without warning. You could use our extra hands, believe me."

"I wish I could believe you—"

"You can, Zeke," said Sylvie. "I've just gotten confirmation from Corlissa Murdock, in orbit. He's legit."

"Good. Sorry, Calvin," Zeke nodded at Marty, who returned the spears and hand lasers to the four Arrs. "Calvin, do you have a weapon?" Zeke asked.

"Yes. A sonic gun over by the crates." Calvin went to get it. "I set it at a moderate level that hurts without doing much damage. So far I haven't really had to injure any Arrs with it. But I do intend to get out of here alive."

"Couldn't agree more," said Jackson, moving to the mouth of the cave to look out. He shook his head. "It sure seems silly for us to be fighting when the whole planet is about to go anyway."

"Just don't hurt them unnecessarily," said Zeke.

"You may as well know now," said Calvin. "We can abide by that, but my Arr companions here have no reservations of that kind." Calvin spoke a few guttural Arr words. The two Arrs holding spears leaned them against the cave wall and moved toward the interior of the cave and came out stringing large bows, with full quivers hanging from thongs wrapped around their waists.

"Pardon my not mentioning those, Dr. Bones," Calvin said casually. "I wasn't going to let you kill us, either, if it came to that."

Zeke gave him a wry smile. "Call me Zeke."

"Here they come," said Sylvie.

Zeke looked out the cave mouth. Arrs were just trotting out of the forest below. Some were filing up the path, while others were spreading out in a line at the edge of the forest.

"About twenty, as Sylvie said," Jackson observed.

"Calvin," said Zeke. "Do you have a plan for defending this cave? How do they attack?"

Calvin came up beside him. "That line at the forest will be archers. They'll try to keep us backed away from the cave mouth while the others storm the cave." He took Zeke's arm and drew him back. "They're starting to shoot."

The cave opening did not offer very much cover from the large arrows that began to fly. The main advantage of the cave was that the terrace in front of it presented an obstacle from below. The Arrs had to arch their arrows over it, which dissipated more of their force, in addition to the obvious disadvantage of shooting uphill.

Zeke and Calvin knelt by one corner of the cave opening, where they could just see the other Arrs, bearing spears and smaller hand weapons, nimbly moving up the path. Jackson and Marty crouched at the other corner, also watching. Sylvie wriggled forward in a prone position near them to get her video recordings of the attack.

Arrows clattered onto the terrace. More struck the outside of the cave, one of them striking a spark that fell and died. Two flew harmlessly into the cave, one of them directly over Sylvie.

Zeke and Jackson fired their lasers below, again aiming over the Arrs' heads. Calvin leaned around Zeke and fired his sonic gun in a sustained blast. A moment later, a large branch fell in front of several Arr archers, making them jump back.

"It won't slow them down long," Calvin muttered.

The four Arrs in the cave were not concerned with cover. All of them stepped right up to the center of the cave mouth in a line. They matched their opponents in courage and concentration.

The two Arrs with hand lasers raked fire right into the line of archers below, and Zeke heard shrieks of pain. The two with bows and arrows were holding small hand bows, not the big ones that Zeke had seen used by Arrs lying on their backs and bracing with their feet. The two in the cave stood calmly as arrows sped by them and released their own arrows in return.

"Calvin," Zeke said quietly. "I don't mind the bows and arrows, I guess, but I hate to have those other two Arrs killing their own kind with lasers. Can you ask them to wait, maybe tell them we'll need them in reserve?"

Calvin shook his head. "They would consider it an insult, a lack of trust in their ability."

"Maybe we could make it up to them somehow later."

"No," said Calvin. "I've paid them in food, weapons, and certain types of stone that are used as currency here to work for me. If we insult them, that won't count for much. They'd quit helping for sure and they might just turn on us."

Zeke scowled and burned his own laser across the path below, just in front of the lead Arr.

Jackson and Marty did the same. The lead Arr stopped, then sprang over the smoking line of grass and moved forward again, hefting a large spear. His companions followed.

"They don't scare easily," said Calvin. "Get ready. I'm not sure what to expect."

"Ten of them in the assault," Zeke counted. "Have you had to kill any before?"

"No." Calvin turned to look at him. "But I wasn't taking their holy relics before, either."

Zeke nodded and picked out another branch down below over the archers. "The ones on their way up are almost here. Let's go after the archers at the bottom one more time before they get here."

"Good idea. You have anything special in mind?" Calvin asked, looking down below.

Zeke fired his laser. "See where I'm firing? Join me and we'll bring it down faster."

The combination of sonic and laser power broke off a sizable branch that came crashing down on the edge of the forest. As before, the Arr archers heard it creaking and had scrambled back before it fell. It threw them into disarray without slaughtering them.

Zeke and Calvin did it again and then a third time.

The line of archers was thrown back, at least for the moment. The four Arrs in the cave turned their attention to the line of Arrs moving up the slope. They had reached the steepest portion of the bluff, just below the terrace of the cave, and had slowed down.

Zeke dialed down the power on his hand laser, catching the eyes of Jackson and Marty. They did likewise, but with expressions of concern. At this level, the weapons would cause a wide surface burn on a living victim, but no more than that.

The two Arrs with hand lasers were still firing at full strength. They had had to return their attention to the archers, who had now regrouped. The Arrs in the cave with bows were focused on the Arrs on the path below, forcing them to spread out.

The approaching Arrs mounted the terrace with a chorus of baying sounds and came running forward. Spears and small hand axes flew and Zeke drew back against the side wall, firing his laser. Now everyone in the cave was shooting point-blank into the assault.

One of the Arrs in the cave fell with a spear in his haunch, screeching. A flurry of hand axes forced Marty and Jackson to back farther into the cave, still firing. Two more heavy spears sailed into the cave as well, striking the stone and dirt floor.

Jackson leaned sideways to grab one of the spears. He rose up and gave it a great heave. The spear flew narrowly over the Arrs' heads and dropped beyond the edge of the terrace.

Zeke knew very well Jackson could have hit one of them if he had tried.

At that, the two Arrs in the cave armed with bows suddenly dropped them and snatched up spears that had been thrown into the cave. Then they suddenly ran forward themselves to meet the stalling attack. The other one grabbed a throwing axe in one hand and kept firing his hand laser with the other as he charged after them.

Zeke kept up his own fire as did the others still in the cave. Then, as quickly as the Arrs had assaulted the terrace, they suddenly broke and ran from the three of their own species rushing at them. Zeke and Calvin stood up, holding their fire. Jackson and Marty also stood up and lowered their weapons.

The fleeing Arrs were ignoring the path as they rushed down the bluff, may of them to tumble and roll much of the way. Their fellows at the bottom, on the edge of the forest, vanished from sight, pulling their casualties with them. The three Arrs from the cave stood on the edge of the terrace whooping and baying and jumping around.

Calvin smiled wryly. "I've never seen them in battle before. Only individual combat over personal disputes."

"Sylvie, did you get all of that?" Zeke asked.

She had rushed forward when the enemy had backed off and was now just behind the three Arrs on the terrace. "Got it, Zeke. Calvin, do you have a first aid kit? For the wounded Arr."

Calvin pointed to a small portable container near the piles of stacked cargo. "It has all you need for a flesh wound like that."

"That video will be important data for the anthropological files," said Zeke. "Take care of it."

"Calvin," said Jackson. "Any idea what they'll do now? Are they likely to regroup and attack again soon, or wait, or what?"

"I'm not certain. Many of their decisions are made in a council, though, so they may have to confer with each other before taking more action."

"We can hope," said Zeke. "All right. Calvin, you said you hadn't seen them in battle before, but you had taken steps to be ready for it. What's going on?"

"I hired these four Arrs to help me salvage what I could and to protect me," said Calvin. "I figured an attack was inevitable, but this is the first one."

"All right, that makes sense."

Calvin hesitated. "You do understand, don't you, that I would never steal sacred symbols and writing from this culture if it wasn't doomed anyway? That's important to me.

"So the bulk of the Arrs down there are just defending their culture and their homes as best they can." Marty shook his head. "I usually like this job, but this time . . ."

Zeke nodded. "Yes, I understand. But I'm not ready to give up yet, either."

Sylvie looked up at him from where she was bandaging the wounded Arr. He lay quietly, appreciative of the attention.

"What do you mean, Zeke?" Calvin asked.

Zeke turned to face him. "I don't want to see these Arrs destroyed and I don't want to see their cultural icons stolen."

"We can't take them anywhere," said Marty. "We don't have the room on board ship or anywhere to take them."

"That's right. We can't take them anywhere." Zeke shook his head. "If I can get that comet diverted, will you restore everything of theirs to its original position?"

Calvin looked at him for a moment. "Sure. *If*. That's a pretty tall order."

"Never mind that. Will you return every artifact you've taken and leave them alone?"

"Absolutely."

"All right," said Zeke, with a firm nod. "I'm going to get that comet diverted myself, somehow. While we're working on that, you start unpacking your containers . . ."

"Wait a minute. Just how sure are you of this?"

"And return everything to its original position the best you can," Zeke finished.

Calvin drew himself up. "Now it's your turn. If I restore all the artifacts, and you fail to divert the comet, will you take responsibility for the loss of all the materials?"

Zeke could feel everyone watching him. He took in a deep breath and let it out. "Send word down to the Arrs that you're returning everything. They'll stop the attacks and let you work in peace."

Chapter Eight

At least, Zeke reflected, he now had a clear idea of what he had to do. He still didn't know who had attacked them or why, but Corlissa Murdock might know. She was still in orbit around Thomsen 4.

Calvin radioed her ship and put Sylvie into contact with Dean Noslich, the communications officer on the *Omaha*. Zeke had Sylvie take down the position of Murdock's orbit so she could enter it into their lander's computer. Sylvie also notified Kadak!xa of their plans to visit Murdock in orbit.

When Sylvie was satisfied that the wounded Arr was not seriously hurt, they left the bluffs. As they departed, Calvin began to explain to his Arr crew that he wanted them to undo all the work they had done in the cave. They had a mixed reaction at best.

The trip back to the lander on foot was extremely tense. Jackson walked point. Sylvie kept a very careful ear attuned for the presence of hostile **ARRS.**

Apparently the group that had attacked them had had enough action for now. Two individual scouts seemed to follow Zeke and his party, but they did not show themselves. The group returned safely to the lander and finally relaxed.

Zeke flew the lander directly up to the *Omaha*, Corlissa Murdock's big invariance overdrive freighter. One of her assistants escorted them to a cozy lounge somewhere in the heart of the great ship.

Zeke settled into a well-padded reclining chair and waited for his companions to make themselves comfortable around an oval of seats and small tables in between them. Paintings labeled to show different horse breeds adorned the walls.

Corlissa Murdock sat down on his left in a similar recliner. She was perhaps forty, with long blond hair drawn back rather severely. An assistant, a slender young man with a full head of wavy brown hair, brought a variety of refreshments to everyone.

Corlissa made small talk with each of her guests until they had all been served. Her assistant moved quickly and courteously among them. When everyone had a drink, the young man left the room. Corlissa turned to Zeke and raised her eyebrows.

"It's a surprise to find anyone as far out on the civilized fringes as Thomsen 4," she said pleasantly. "But Calvin recently told my people by radio that you were still hoping to save the planet somehow. What do you have in mind?"

"I'm still trying to catch up on my information," said Zeke. "I seem to have jumped into this whole situation without knowing exactly where matters stand."

"What do you mean?"

"For instance," said Zeke, "I understand that you were planning to divert the comet as a prelude to developing the planet. Calvin says that's no longer the case."

"I was." Corlissa sighed. "But now my business is in trouble from top to bottom. I just came out from Earth to pick up Calvin and his salvage because no one could get him without BEC's IO to make the trip. Not that many of us have it. But I can't afford much time out here."

"I still want to know why you can't, or won't, divert the comet." Zeke sipped his drink.

She raised an eyebrow. "I thought I just answered that. If you're asking for private details about my business matters, I don't feel that sharing them is necessary."

Zeke shook his head. "Of course not. I'm asking about the logistics of moving the comet. Specifically."

"All right. It's a huge comet, too big to divert even with licensed atomics."

"That's not the only way to move a comet," said Marty gruffly, at the far end of the oval.

"What about hitting it with other planetoids?" Jackson asked. "It doesn't have to be moved very much."

"That would mean months of flying around planting the right charges in various planetoids," Corlissa explained. "Invariance overdrive wouldn't work at such short distances and I can't afford the fuel or the time to go chasing around this solar system on regular drive."

"It's not a high price to pay for saving an entire intelligent species and its culture," said Zeke. "I might be able to help out with expenses through a foundation I established if you can help with your facilities."

"That's very generous, but—"

"Your ship would make a big difference. Two of us can do it in only half the time. As you noticed, it's not exactly crowded around here."

"It's not just the money." Corlissa shook her head apologetically. "I can't spend the time away from my other commitments. I have my limits, too."

Zeke nodded thoughtfully, gazing into his glass. He couldn't ask her to ruin her business on Earth while she was out here. A glance at his companions told him that they understood, though they were as disappointed as he was.

"You know . . . I might have a little more information you could use," she said slowly. "It's not much."

"Anything would help." Zeke sighed.

"Well, you know the name of Peter Chrysanthi?"

Jackson sat up.

Zeke stiffened. "Yes. Why?"

"He's the one who pulled strings to put pressure on me. A number of my clients have demanded services all at once, while creditors have begun calling in loans."

"What is your history with him?" Zeke asked. Chrysanthi was an old adversary of his, dating all the way back to the time Chrysanthi had been allied with Bart Charles in their failed attempt to take over Bones Energy Corporation. They had crossed paths from time to time since then.

"None," said Corlissa. "But I suppose he might have an interest in Thomsen 4."

"Why?" Jackson asked. "If everyone else has left it alone for this long?"

"After all, it is very Earthlike. Developers could make it very profitable, as long as they have the money to buy an invariance overdrive ship from your company."

"Not very many can afford it," said Zeke. "Chrysanthi is one of those who can."

"Would the planet be worth developing even after the comet hits?" Jackson demanded.

"Quite likely. A ship without IO would arrive after the dust cloud had settled and the cometary winter had ended."

"What about your competition in this area of space?" Zeke asked. "Let's consider that line of argument."

"Actually, I was surprised to find that no other developers were pursuing projects in the Thomsen System," said Corlissa. "A planet this Earthlike is worth a great deal."

"I should think so," said Marty.

Corlissa smiled wryly. "Now I wonder if Chrysanthi has something to do with it."

"So you think maybe he bought them off or stopped them some other way before they even got started?" Zeke asked.

"It seems likely to me." She shrugged. "I suppose he just got around to me last, after I had dropped off Calvin to start his research and cataloguing. My best guess is that he was out here first, just ahead of me."

"Could his information about the Thomsen solar system be more thorough than yours?" Marty asked.

"It's possible," she answered. "We've been very distracted out here this trip, to be honest."

A red light appeared on the little table between Zeke and Corlissa. She pulled out a private earphone on a retracting cord and listened for a moment.

Zeke lifted his drink, then paused to look around the lounge. The paintings represented a number of different breeds of horse rendered in a Victorian style. The paintings were originals, though he could not tell from a distance when they had been painted. Murdock had done very well, at least well enough to equip this immense freighter with invariance overdrive. If she said her business was in trouble, then apparently she knew what she was talking about.

Corlissa let the earphone retract with a snap and stood up. "I have an emergency on the bridge. Dr. Bones—"

"Zeke."

"Zeke, I'd like you to accompany me, but this is no time for a crowd. Would your crew mind— "

"Waiting here? We're your guests, after all." Zeke rose and turned to the others. "Relax here, eh?"

"I'll start reviewing some of the data I've collected," said Sylvie, setting down her glass.

"Thank you," said Corlissa. "I'll send someone back in to see if you need anything. Zeke, this way."

Zeke followed her through the ship.

"I've been informed that another ship has approached us with evasive maneuvers. My captain suspects it is hostile and he is preparing for an attack."

Zeke began to fill her in on the attacks he had endured since leaving New Yale. She was surprised, but agreed with him that Thomsen 4 was somehow the common denominator of all the hostilities. By the time they had reached the bridge, she had been brought up to date.

The bridge was small, hardly more than a cockpit, and staffed by only two members, a Captain Eloresem, and the communications officer, Dean Noslich, according to the briefing Sylvie had given Zeke back on the *Ostrom*. They would both be qualified to pilot the ship when they were not relying on the computer, Zeke realized. Corlissa had more important concerns than driving the ship.

He and Corlissa had to stand in the small space between the two seats.

"Status, Eldon," said Corlissa.

"That's it on the screen," said Captain Eloresem. "No response to our hailing, no regular flight pattern. It's continuing to use evasive measures as it comes closer."

"But they haven't fired on us yet?"

"No, not yet."

Zeke glanced at the strip of written data running below the screen. It gave the estimated distance of the other ship, changing rapidly as it approached. "They could have fired a lot sooner, before you even noticed them."

"You think they want to be seen first?" Corlissa asked, still watching the screen.

"I'm sure of it."

"They're firing," said Captain Eloresem. He tapped the keys on the console in front of him. "Standard missiles coming in straight. Our computer is countering with laser fire to detonate them in space." He shook his head. "We're picking 'em off easily."

"Contact the *Ostrom*," said Zeke. "It's in orbit here someplace. Maybe we can squeeze our mysterious visitors a little between us." He gave Noslich a scramble code to use so the enemy would not pick up the communication.

Corlissa turned to Noslich. "Go ahead."

Zeke nodded toward the screen. "It was the same when they attacked us. We defended ourselves easily, almost as though they had set it up that way."

"I have the *Ostrom*, boss," said Noslich. "I'll put it on the speaker."

"Kadak!xa, Zeke here."

"Copy."

"Have you located us—the *Omaha* and an unidentified hostile ship?" he asked.

"The computer is just bringing in the coordinates now, based on the communications signal. You're on the far side of the planet from me at the moment. Instructions?"

"Close in as fast as you can. See if you can land a few shots. If we can't disable the enemy, maybe we can force them to show more cards than they want."

"We'll try to keep them distracted," said Corlissa. "Eldon, step up our own maneuvers. Keep them jumping."

"Good move," said Zeke.

"I'll turn it over to the computer," Captain Eloresem said.

"They're stepping up the attack, adding particle beams," said Noslich. "I'm dropping the communication for now."

"Boss," said Captain Eloresem. "Our shields are up, but I recommend strapping in right away."

"Come on," said Corlissa. "My office has seats we can use. I'll patch into the bridge screens from there."

Zeke followed her quickly. They were still jogging down a short hallway when the ship vibrated hard and took a change in direction sharp enough to throw them against the wall. A moment later, they were strapping into seats in Corlissa's office.

They sat for some time without speaking as the ship maneuvered in response to the computer. The new positions were reflected in the relationships represented on the wall screen. The enemy ship was a red dot in the center. Finally a new speck of white light appeared in the far corner.

"There," said Zeke. "That's the *Ostrom*."

Suddenly the red speck in the center vanished.

"Hey," said Corlissa, sitting up against the restraining belt. "What happened?"

"Invisibility shields," said Zeke grimly. "Not exactly cheap. This is some ship we're dealing with."

"Invisibility shields! You didn't mention them before, Zeke." She turned to look at him.

"They didn't use them before."

"You mean there is more than one enemy ship out here? People only came out to this system after the publicity on Earth from my first visit. That means every ship that has reached the Thomsen System in such a short time had to use IO to get here—just how much money can they have backing them?" She was appalled.

The ship vibrated again with another hit of some kind on its shields and Zeke waited it out.

"I don't believe anybody out here can afford two IO ships," said Zeke. "Maybe they have one ship and they've been holding their identifying characteristics close to the vest."

"What for?"

"To make it look like more than one ship, maybe. Or just to keep us guessing."

"They've succeeded," she said through clenched teeth, as the ship vibrated hard again. "I don't have anything like that. We're a sitting duck if they can see us and we can't see them."

"Keep watching." Zeke followed the movements of light on the screen as the *Ostrom* also took evasive action and sent out a spray of missiles and particle beams in the hope of hitting the undetected enemy, yet missing the *Omaha*.

"No response," said Corlissa, after a moment.

Zeke looked over the screen. The enemy ship had not fired back or reappeared.

"Think they're gone?" she asked.

"No telling. It fits the pattern, though. They put up a weak attack, draw a response, then run."

They waited a little longer. Finally Captain Eloresem called Corlissa.

"I've conferred with the *Ostrom*, and we both are pretty sure that the enemy has withdrawn," he said.

"*How* certain are you?" she demanded.

"We don't have any guarantees," he answered. "They could be playing possum right next to us, for that matter. But we can't operate on that assumption indefinitely."

"All right." Corlissa began to unstrap.

"I'm betting the enemy has withdrawn for the moment," said Zeke. "We'll get back to the *Ostrom*. Right away."

The flight in the lander from the *Omaha* back to the safety of the *Ostrom* was somewhat like the long trek on the surface of the planet from the cave back to the lander. Everyone was tense, on edge, aware of their vulnerability to a largely unknown enemy . . . but nothing happened. Zeke was sure that the purpose of these attacks was to divert them or keep them busy. If something more serious had been intended right now, the little lander would have been too tempting a target to ignore.

As Zeke bounded onto the bridge in the welcome confines of the *Ostrom*, Kadak!xa turned her great bulk toward him.

"Welcome back, Zeke," she said. "Had some excitement while you were gone, eh?"

He winked. "Glad to be back in one piece."

"Ain't that the truth," said Marty, shaking his head as he followed Zeke.

Sylvie slid into her seat without a word and began moving all the data she had collected into the ship computer.

"We still have a lot of work to do," said Jackson. "But it's been a very long day."

"Good point," said Zeke. "I'm still wide awake, so why doesn't everyone else retire for the night? I'll sit up for a bit."

Sylvie was the last to leave the bridge. After entering her new data, she asked the computer to correlate all its information for clues to the identity of the enemy ship and for all the options available for diverting the comet. Then she, too, went to bed.

Zeke leaned back with a sigh. He had gathered a lot of information today but so far it hadn't led very far.

The board lit up telling him he had a call from off the ship. Surprised, he reached over to answer.

"Zeke? Corlissa Murdock."

"What's up?"

"I have a security staff here on the *Omaha* and we turned up something. Not a lot, maybe—"

"What happened?"

"It turns out that a new employee of mine, the one who served refreshments to us in the lounge, made a transmission from the *Omaha* right after he left us."

"Really?"

"I have to apologize. Apparently I hired someone planted by Chrysanthi or someone involved with him. His call gave away your presence here and of course allowed the other ship to home on the signal for our position."

"And this guy has been serving you right along, in a position to overhear all your conversations?"

"A good many of them." She hesitated. "The truth is, that's a pretty low-level job. Starting someone new there has been standard practice for me. When I hired him, I didn't know I had an enemy to worry about."

"Fair enough, Corlissa. Thanks." Zeke broke contact and closed his eyes. He was just glad he had not discussed his possible plans in more detail with her.

Chapter Nine

The next morning, Zeke reclined on the bridge, looking over the correlated data in the computer. Marty stood looking over Sylvie's shoulder at her screen, discussing the same data Zeke was reviewing.

"What do you think, Marty?" Zeke asked, waving a hand at the screen in front of him. "Sylvie?"

"We don't have much to go on, Zeke," said Marty. "You know what, though.

"Yeah?"

"We have a fair amount of data on the ship that keeps attacking us." Marty stood up straight and frowned at the floor, thinking.

"But not enough to identify it?"

"Almost enough. The problem is, we were never ready for it when it attacked."

"That's the nature of sneak attacks, isn't it? What are you getting at?"

"Suppose we draw another attack somehow, only this time we're ready with our scanners."

"What information can we get that way that we don't already have?" Zeke asked.

"If we're ready, we can judge appearance, energy consumption, mass, volume..." Marty shrugged. "You name it."

"Not if they use those invisibility shields to block our sensors," said Zeke.

"If you're right that they want to distract us," said Sylvie, "then they can't afford to stay invisible."

"True." Zeke nodded. "They will have to make themselves visible at least long enough to get our attention."

"We won't need much time if we're ready," said Marty. "How 'bout it, Zeke?"

Zeke blanked the screen full of numbers and spun his seat around. "It sounds good."

"How are we going to induce an attack?" Jackson asked from the doorway.

"I was just thinking," said Zeke. "We'll need some precise analyses of that big comet anyway."

"Excellent," said Marty. "Suppose we head out to double-check *its* mass, composition, orbit . . . everything."

Jackson grinned. "Right. It's a good bet our . . . *friends* . . . will keep us company on that trip."

"Let's do it," said Zeke. "Marty, set the sensors the way you want them now. They could attack any time."

Marty got to work on it, conferring with Sylvie to coordinate with the data she had already gathered.

Zeke turned to Kadak!xa. "Kadak!xa, find that comet and plot a course out to it. And when you have it, break orbit and go."

She turned back to her console.

Zeke started to turn away, then hesitated. "Kadak!xa, take us out there at a fast speed, but one well below maximum."

She looked at him questioningly.

"We want to make sure the other ship will have time to notice us and catch up without our being too obvious about it."

"Of course."

The trip out to the comet took a number of days, cutting across the plane of the comet's orbit at a significant boost. No sign of the other ship was detected. Marty speculated that the enemy ship was following them with its invisibility shields up until it chose to attack.

The *Ostrom* moved into a position alongside the comet at a comfortable distance and maintained it. The data necessary for the analyses was gathered on the way, of course, in almost no time once the *Ostrom* was close enough to the comet. Nothing unexpected showed up in the technical data from the comet, but they were all reassured that if they could find a way to divert it, at least they could plan the diversion effectively.

The other ship had not shown itself, however. Zeke was puzzled by its absence.

"How long do you want to stay out here with the comet?" Jackson asked, gazing at it on one of the bridge screens.

"Looking at it up close was fun for a while," said Marty. "But now what?"

Zeke sighed. "I guess if we stay any longer we'll be wasting time we can't afford."

"That's my feeling, Zeke," said Jackson.

"I was pretty sure this would draw some attention from that ship," said Zeke.

"Maybe they don't mind our being out here," said Sylvie. "Maybe they'd rather have us here than on the planet."

Jackson nodded grimly.

"And maybe," Marty growled, "they're hard at work on the planet themselves. How 'bout it, Zeke?"

Kadak!xa gave her slow nod. "Time to head back?"

Zeke turned to look at Marty's solid, rocklike face, then Kadak!xa's great hooded shape. "Yeah. Yeah, I guess we'd better."

"I'll take it," said Jackson, turning to the computer. "Course for Thomsen 4."

"Fine," said Zeke absently. "But why wouldn't they be concerned about our looking at the comet?"

The answer arrived only a few moments after the *Ostrom* changed course for the planet.

"Zeke!" Sylvie called excitedly. "I've got that ship on screen, coming in fast."

"Ha!" Zeke pounded his fist on the arm of his seat. "So they have been watching us."

"Behind their invisibility shields," said Marty, looking at one of the screens. "Just like I said."

"Or else they just got here," said Sylvie. "Either way, they're opening the same as before—missiles."

"We'll defend the same as before," said Zeke. "Jackson?"

"I've already given it to the computer," said Jackson. "Defensive lasers are up now."

"Marty?" Zeke asked. "Are you getting the data on the ship you wanted?"

Marty actually grinned. "It's flowing in like a waterfall —whoops, there they go."

The enemy ship had once again turned and fled, but it was still visible on screen.

"They're heading away from Thomsen 4," Zeke observed. "Somehow I'm not surprised."

"Follow 'em, Zeke?" Jackson asked. "Or..."

"Got all you need, Marty?" Zeke asked.

"We have all we can get this way, I'd say," said Marty. "Close to it, anyway."

"You sure?"

"Probably," he said apologetically. "I won't really know till we have time to review it."

"Let's get back to Thomsen 4," said Zeke. "Right now. Something new must be going on there now."

"Something that this ship wants hidden from us," Sylvie agreed, her jewelry dangling as she nodded.

"We're on our way," said Jackson.

"Higher speed this time," Zeke added. "High-gee boost. Preparations, everybody."

"Give me two minutes, Ezekiel," said Marty. "Hmm— no, it's coming in now."

"What is it? What do you have?"

"It's coming on your screen now, Zeke," said Marty. "Sylvie, do you agree with the conclusions here? I do."

Sylvie nodded. "So do I. It looks like Peter Chrysanthi's ship to me, too."

Zeke studied the readout in front of him.

"The size, shape, mass, fuel consumption . . . the list has all the main features," said Marty.

"Everything matches up to the last ship we know Peter Chrysanthi to have used," said Zeke quietly.

"Appears to be the case," said Marty.

"Including the invariance overdrive it must have had to get to the Thomsen System," said Sylvie.

Zeke continued reading. "The maneuvers, the weaponry . . . everything fits."

"Chrysanthi," Jackson muttered to himself, shaking his head. "It figures."

"Of all people," Zeke agreed. "Let's get underway."

The first half of the trip back to the planet under high acceleration was stressful but necessary. Individually, they only had the energy for required ship communication and with the computer flying the ship that was virtually nonexistent. Deceleration in the second half was not much more comfortable. The enemy ship did not show itself and, Zeke hoped, had been left behind at least for a short time.

The crew let the idle chatter wait for more pleasant circumstances. Zeke found himself pondering the puzzle of Chrysanthi's motives quietly to himself. He suspected the others, who were also limiting their movements as much as possible, were doing the same.

This return trip took fewer days than the journey out to the comet, but it felt longer under the circumstances. At least, Zeke reflected, no one was shooting at them. Finally the computer announced that they were back in orbit around Thomsen 4.

"Sometimes I think I'd rather be shot at than boost that hard," Marty muttered. "Well, at least it's over."

"Personally," said Jackson, "I'd rather boost than be shot at. But now what, Zeke? Down to the planet?"

"Yes, but first I have a question," said Zeke.

"What is it?" Kadak!xa asked.

"I've been thinking about Chrysanthi the whole trip back and I've got one contradiction about him I can't figure out."

"What?" Sylvie asked.

"The most likely reason for anyone from Earth to be interested in Thomsen 4 is that it's ideal for human habitation," said Zeke. "Isn't that right?"

"As far as we know," Kadak!xa cautioned. "Our data is still pretty thin."

"All right, as far as we know. But if Chrysanthi wants to squeeze out other developers so he can take it over, why does he want the comet to hit and create a planet-wide disaster? Why not start developing now instead of waiting for the dust cloud to settle?"

"Yeah," said Jackson. "I've been thinking about that, too. The question is, why is he trying to insure that the comet hits the planet if he wants the resources of the planet for himself?"

"I can't figure out what he would gain from letting the comet hit," said Zeke. "But if he's out here to make sure it does, he must have some stake in it."

"His infamous gambling," said Jackson. "If he's not compulsive about it, he's close. Maybe he's got some kind of action on the collision."

"Who would bet against him?" Zeke asked. "Whether or not a comet is going to hit a planet in a star system far from Earth doesn't sound like it would attract a big following."

"I vote for getting down to the planet," said Jackson. "Everything seems to center around it."

"Fair enough," said Zeke. "Does anyone else have any theories about Chrysanthi?"

Kadak!xa shook her great head.

"Not enough data, Zeke," said Sylvie.

"All right," said Zeke. "Jackson and Kadak!xa, come down to the planet with me."

"Equip yourselves better this time," said Marty.

"Definitely," said Zeke. "We'll need armor against the Arrs' weapons, but go easy on our firepower."

"Sonic and laser sidearms and rifles like before," Jackson suggested. "No other weapons."

"Some climbing equipment," Zeke added. "Anything of use in a forest or on the bluffs. Just don't load us down too much. We'll have to move quickly on foot."

Jackson and Kadak!xa went to suit up.

"Marty," said Zeke. "I want you to stay here and work on a way for us to divert the comet using just the *Ostrom*."

"Can't be done."

Zeke grinned. "You always give me that kind of talk, old friend. And you always come through."

Marty scowled at him.

"Work on it, all right?" Zeke gave him a playful punch on his rocklike shoulder.

"Zeke."

"What?"

"It's not just a complaint this time."

"What do you mean?"

"We're working with certain constants here— momentum and a limited number of resources with a short deadline."

"Yes?"

"We need a certain amount of energy to move that comet from its orbit and the longer we take, the more we need," said Marty. "No amount of argument will change that. I can't just invent a new machine or something, or discover a previously unknown architectural use for an alien crystal form."

"I remember my physics, Marty," Zeke said with a grin. "See what you can come up with."

Marty turned away, shaking his head. "The Thomsen System has so many comets and planetoids in it anyway. If this comet doesn't hit the planet, maybe one of the next few hundred will."

Sylvie caught Zeke's eye and smiled. They both knew that if the *Ostrom* could move that comet somehow, Marty would figure out a way to do it.

"I was thinking, Zeke," said Sylvie. "Maybe I could review my records and find some clue to what Chrysanthi is up to."

"Good idea."

"If I come up with something while you're on the planet, is it okay if I try countermoves of my own? I may need your name here and there," she explained.

"Of course. I'll back whatever you decide will help." He winked and went to Jackson and Kadak!xa.

Zeke flew the three of them down in the winged lander. They skimmed the treetops as Zeke looked for a landing site closer to the cave in the bluffs. He wanted to avoid another land march through hostile Arr territory if he could.

"This is pretty country," said Kadak!xa. "But heavily forested. Perhaps the top of the bluffs offer enough clear space to land. Or have you tried there?"

"No, I haven't," said Zeke. "I'll circle back and take a look." He began to bank gently. "On the way, I'll show you Calvin Louie's little ship fortress."

The lander took a long curve that would carry them to the bluffs. Ahead, Zeke could see the dot on a raised clearing that was Calvin's ship.

"Down there," he said. He and Jackson had briefed Kadak!xa on the finer points of their first visit on the way down from orbit.

"Something's wrong, Zeke," said Jackson, as they drew nearer the site below.

"What?"

"That energy fence. It's gone. Or to be exact, the ship's not putting it out any more."

Zeke altered course into a tight circle over the site and looked down. Jackson was right. The lander sat on the little hilltop alone with marks of damage on it.

"What does that look like to you?" Zeke asked.

"Laser fire maybe," said Jackson. "At this distance, it's hard to be sure."

"The door is standing open," said Kadak!xa. "It must be deserted, probably looted."

"Calvin gave hand lasers to two of his Arrs," Zeke mused. "They don't have the power to do this, or the inclination."

Jackson picked up the communicator and tried unsuccessfully to raise a response. "I didn't expect anybody."

By this time Zeke was flying directly for the top of the bluffs. "We have to get to the cave. If someone else has landed, that's where they'll be."

The front of the bluffs presented a fairly flat cliff face. This was the side that Zeke's party had approached before. The top of these bluffs was rocky and unevenly forested, offering no area for them to land. However, the top surface sloped gently back from the front edge of the cliff. Zeke spied a narrow strip where he thought he could just barely bring the lander down.

The winged lander came in at a low angle over the tree-tops as Zeke looked for the open strip.

"You sure about this?" Jackson asked. "Not that I'm doubting your ability, but..."

"This is no worse than that strip by your lousy art gallery in the Ozarks," Zeke said with a grin. "Here we go."

The trees flew by on both sides as the lander descended gradually, closer than even Zeke had anticipated. The lander came to a safe halt, however, slowed in part by the uphill angle of the natural landing strip. Zeke then turned the lander around so it would be positioned for a quick takeoff later.

They climbed out of the lander, Kadak!xa bringing the ropes and clamps that Jackson had brought on board. "I believe you will want these," she said.

Zeke and Jackson began preparing the rappeling equipment. Kadak!xa's body would not allow her to rappel down the cliff with human equipment.

"I looked over the bluff when we flew in," said Kadak!xa. "I know where the cave is."

"All right," said Zeke. "Did you see a route you can take around the side of the bluff?"

"I believe so. Since I do not know the exact configuration of the cave, burrowing directly into the ground to meet would be a waste of time. If I cannot reach the cave, I will wait for you here," she said. She turned and began moving through the sparse trees on the top of the bluff.

Zeke and Jackson started straight for the edge of the cliff.

Chapter Ten

Near the edge of the cliff, Zeke set down their coil of rope. He and Jackson dropped to their bellies. Then they crawled quietly across the uneven rock surface to the very edge of the cliff.

Short, crooked bushes grew out of the rock here and there all the way down. The rock was cracked and broken with many jagged outcroppings and loose stones. They could climb back up if necessary.

They peered over the side, careful not to dislodge any debris that would reveal their presence to anyone. The cave was below and to their right. Kadak!xa had not yet had time to reach the cliff, even if she could find a way.

They could not see any sign of activity but the distinct sound of many rock saws buzzed and whined from the cave. Zeke turned and looked at Jackson in silent agreement.

They would have to see who was in the cave. Knowing exactly what the intruders were doing, and how many were present, was crucial. Obviously, they had to avoid revealing themselves as they reconnoitered, if that was possible.

Jackson pointed to a small open spot at the base of the cliff. It was hidden from the cave mouth by a couple of short, twisted trees. Zeke nodded and they withdrew from the edge.

Without a word, they uncoiled one long rope. Normally they would use a safety line left tied to a tree on top of the cliff. Zeke did not dare use one now lest that rope be seen by the enemy.

Instead, they would have to rappel down the cliff the way the original rock and mountain climbers had long ago, leaving nothing behind.

Zeke hung the middle of the rope around the trunk of a tree. Jackson threw both ends down the cliff to their destination. Then they donned their gloves and stepped into their seat rigs. They clipped the rectangular rings on their seat rigs over the double length of rope. Zeke was going first, so he turned his back to the precipice, hoisted the rope back over his shoulder, and kicked off the edge of the cliff.

This was the most vulnerable time for them. If an enemy from the cave or the forest happened to look their way, they would be visible, helpless targets who would not even see a shot in the back coming. They had to get down the cliff as fast as possible.

As Zeke kicked, the motion also sent him sliding down the rope. He swung back toward the cliff, cushioned the impact with his legs, and kicked off again. With two more kicks, he had dropped all the way to the ground.

He stepped out of the equipment and waved at Jackson.

His big partner came bouncing down the cliffside even faster, his powerful long legs providing longer kicks. As soon as he landed, they crouched behind the short trees and took one end of the rope. They pulled hand over hand together, drawing the other end of the rope up the cliff and around the tree trunk so it would fall down to them.

Jackson coiled it quickly as they both looked around. No one was evident. The sound of the saws was louder, of course, and now they could hear an unintelligible undertone of shouted orders.

Zeke pointed to a route they could use to crawl toward the terrace of the cave. It afforded cover both from the forest below and from the cave. Once they were near the cave terrace, however, they would have to improvise.

Jackson threw the coil of rope over one shoulder and nodded agreement. He stashed the rest of the rappeling equipment into the big pockets of his fatigues. Then Zeke began a slow, careful crawl toward the cave.

They reached the edge of the raised terrace outside the mouth of the cave without detection. They were still hidden from those inside. Zeke slowly raised his head to look.

It was crowded with strangers, all wearing forest green work suits trimmed with Chrysanthi logo patches. The cave walls near the mouth had been completely denuded of the Arr artifacts that had been painted and sculpted in low relief there. Huge stacks of sealed cartons betrayed their new fate.

Now the crew was cutting out artifacts from deeper in the outer chamber, using lights.

Everyone was busy some distance into the interior. Zeke motioned for Jackson to look also. No one in the cave was likely to see them unless one of the crew happened to walk to the cave mouth for some reason. Jackson raised his head cautiously.

Calvin was not visible, nor was any of his equipment. Zeke saw no sign of any Arrs, either. The cave had been taken over and was being raided for its loot.

Zeke and Jackson could easily get the drop on the people who were visible here. However, Zeke did not dare attack until he knew the size and whereabouts of the entire enemy landing party. His greatest advantage against them would be surprise, and right now he could not afford to give that up.

Zeke and Jackson lowered themselves out of sight and turned to lean with their backs against the side of the terrace.

"We'll need a new base of operations," Zeke said softly, under the whine of the rock saws.

Jackson started to reply, then stopped. He was looking into the distance in the direction from which they had come. Zeke followed his gaze.

Low to the ground, among the short trees and infrequent bushes growing along the base of the cliff, Kadak!xa could just barely be seen. She was moving slowly, aware that the cover was not adequate to hide someone her size.

She was less visible than they had been when they had rappeled down the cliff. On the other hand, she would be partially visible for a much longer time. They had to find a place to go.

Zeke looked up and saw a couple of small cave openings a short distance above Kadak!xa. They had terraces in front of them and narrow, barely visible paths leading to them. He judged that they too were or had been inhabited by Arrs.

Kadak!xa could get up those paths. Zeke nudged Jackson gently and pointed to them. "What do you think?"

Jackson saw the caves and nodded. Zeke began leading the way back to Kadak!xa.

Every so often they paused to look behind them. The cliff and the forest below remained unchanged. They crawled quickly, now more concerned with being seen than with anyone hearing them.

They rejoined Kadak!xa on the path. No one in the work crew had left the cave. Unless they had been seen by someone in the forest, they were still unnoticed.

"Strangers are raiding the cave," Zeke said softly.

"Chrysanthi's people?" Kadak!xa asked.

"I'm certain of it," said Jackson. "But there's no sign of Calvin or the Arrs."

"We're going to try those caves," said Zeke, pointing. "We'll have to approach them carefully in case Chrysanthi's bunch has someone surveying or something, but I don't hear any saws up there."

Kadak!xa nodded agreement.

The three of them began the ascent up the path. Zeke looked out over the forest below the bluff with concern. Anyone could be watching them from there in complete secrecy.

Jackson saw him and shook his head. "If one of Chrysanthi's employees had seen us, an alarm would have been raised," he said with a wry grin.

"Yeah, you're right," said Zeke. "They aren't a very subtle group, are they?"

They cautiously approached the silent caves and peeked into each one. The caves were all deserted but each one exhibited at least some evidence of Arr habitation. Zeke was certain the Arrs had evacuated recently, perhaps earlier that day.

He chose the last cave for their base camp. It was large enough for Jackson to stand and for Kadak!xa to move comfortably. Also, it commanded enough height to offer a good view of the bluff and forest below.

They were close enough to the lander to make a fast escape if necessary, though reaching it would be difficult. Climbing up the cliff again was possible but slow. Taking Kadak!xa's route back would be much easier.

"We'll need to bring some supplies from the lander," said Zeke. "Including spelunking equipment and more rations. One trip will do for the moment."

"Let's wait for nightfall," said Jackson. "Their crew won't see us then."

Zeke shook his head. "Sound will still carry at night and we can't be completely quiet. If they're camping right in that cave, they're more likely to hear us at night when they quit working."

"I agree," said Kadak!xa, nodding her great hood. "We should bring down the supplies and move about on the bluff now while they are occupied inside that cavern."

"I'll go with you, then," said Jackson. "Maybe I can help keep you out of sight."

"All right," said Kadak!xa. "I can lower the supplies directly to the cave on ropes and then retract the ropes again. It will save time and reduce the risk of being seen."

"Did you have much trouble getting around to this side of the bluff?" Zeke asked.

"No," said Kadak!xa. "My route around the side of the bluff is time-consuming but not difficult. Some sort of rockslide brought down much of the cliff and provided a slope I can use."

"Let's go," said Jackson. "I want to look over that route in case we need it later."

"All right," said Zeke, looking at the markings on the cave walls. They were not as elaborate or numerous as those in the cave that was being looted.

Kadak!xa hesitated. "Should I call Sylvie down to record this Arr data?"

"Hmm?" Zeke turned back to her, distracted. "Oh—no. If she can figure out a way to save the planet, we'll have plenty of time to record this later."

"We'll get going," said Jackson. "I'll camouflage the lander while I'm up there. Tell you what, though. We don't want to use any radio communication that the enemy might pick up."

"Right," said Zeke. "When you're ready to lower the supplies, make sure no one's watching the best you can. Then drop a few pebbles on the cave terrace to get my attention."

Jackson nodded and followed Kadak!xa out of the cave.

If they were all careful, Zeke reflected, they could escape notice from the work crew in the other cavern. Apparently the sound of the rock saws had already prevented them from hearing the lander fly nearby. On the other hand, he did not want to get overconfident.

He turned away from the wall artifacts and began a careful search of the portion of the cave that was lit from the entrance. The floor was solid, roughly level, and also showed signs of long habitation in the debris partly buried in it.

Toward the back of the lit area he began to find some small, loose rocks. The floor here was rougher, suggesting less foot traffic. A short distance further, the cavern narrowed and separated into branches.

Some openings were much larger than others. The presence of loose debris suggested to him that the Arrs had only used the outer room of the cave. A couple of wall scratches and footprints in the damp earth suggested perfunctory trips by them into the inner chambers, but he saw no sign that they had come back here regularly.

Perhaps they had ignored this chamber and gone farther back.

He began picking up the loose rocks and looking them over. Then he ran his hand along some of the rock wall. These were ordinary limestone caves, probably honeycombing the cliff with passages of various sizes. Of course, he was too professional to go exploring without the right equipment and companions. Serious fieldwork would have to wait until the comet had been diverted.

Some time later, a tapping sound outside the cave drew his attention. He looked, and a second pebble bounced across the cave terrace from above. After a quick glance around the bluff, he stepped outside the cave and looked up.

Jackson was standing at the edge of the cliff, one foot resting on a large rectangular supply crate sturdily bound with rope. Kadak!xa was out of sight, presumably braced somewhere to lower the crate on the rope. Jackson waved.

Zeke waved back and watched as the crate began to lower. Jackson directed Kadak!xa as it descended. The crate got caught on a small outcropping once and had to be raised again. Otherwise, the descent was smooth if slow.

"Zeke!" Jackson shouted suddenly.

The crate was still about nine meters above Zeke's head. Jackson was pointing behind him.

Zeke looked around and saw a line of Chrysanthi workers standing just outside the cave they had been looting, watching the crate lower. On the path below, a long line of armed Chrysanthi people were moving forward, starting to spread out.

"Get inside!" Jackson yelled.

Zeke knew what was coming. He skipped inside the cave just before the crate came crashing down, the loose rope following right after it. Laser fire began to hit the rock wall around him as he wriggled out low to pull it inside.

The end of another rope dropped to the terrace as he began moving the crate inside the cave. The enemy below suddenly scattered as they became the targets of laser fire from the top of the cliff. That would be Kadak!xa firing, Zeke realized, to cover Jackson as he rappeled down the cliff to join him as fast as possible.

Zeke got the crate inside as Jackson hit the cave terrace, rolled, and skittered inside.

"Kadak!xa will try to join us by the other route," Jackson said grimly, as he swung his laser rifle into position. "Laser on high, Zeke? We aren't fighting Arrs with spears now."

"Avoid killing anybody if you can." Zeke raised the power on his own hand weapon and they fired back at the enemy below.

"Wish we had some real firepower," Jackson muttered.

They were able to slow down the advance of the enemy largely by the advantage of altitude. Zeke guessed that maybe fifty people were in the attack squad, though, and they kept spreading out, advancing, giving each other cover. Jackson and Zeke had no way to stop them.

The brush on the lower portion of the bluff was sparse and the combined laser fire of Jackson and Zeke brought down some of the small trees the enemy could have used otherwise. Jackson pulled out a small sonic gun and started little rockslides with the vibrations in the loose gravel. It was not extremely effective, but it interfered some with the enemy's advance.

Kadak!xa announced her presence with cross fire from her own laser rifle. Several of the enemy went down. Zeke and Jackson could not actually see her without exposing themselves to enemy fire. As she came on, the advance of the enemy stalled as they reacted in surprise to the presence of a !xaka! on the planet.

Kadak!xa's cross fire allowed Zeke and Jackson to force back the enemy in several places. The enemy commander shouted several orders. When the enemy pulled back to regroup, Kadak!xa received enough cover fire to rush along the bluff to the cave terrace, arriving much faster than Zeke had guessed she could.

The enemy began to fire again just as she moved up onto the terrace. Zeke and Jackson covered her with more fire of their own.

Zeke and Jackson backed up to allow her space to enter. For a moment, she seemed to fill the mouth of the cave as she maneuvered her long body, then she again lowered her big hood and moved safely inside the cave.

Zeke started to fire, then hit the floor of the cave just as several lines of laser fire angled into the cave over his head. Some of the rock outside the cave cracked and chipped from the inaudible vibrations of sonic guns.

Kadak!xa settled down on the floor of the cave and began taking careful aim as she fired. Jackson was forced back from the cave mouth by the intensity of enemy fire, but continued to shoot. Zeke moved safely into the cave and opened the crate.

"Calling for help, Zeke?" Jackson asked.

"No, I—"

"What?"

"I don't want them to intercept a transmission. They've certainly identified us, but this fight isn't over yet."

Jackson gritted his teeth and fired again. "I never said it was, did I, Zeke?"

"I want them to waste as much time and resources on us as possible." Zeke was taking some basic spelunking equipment out of the crate. "We'll draw them deeper into the cave, fighting all the way."

"How deep does it go?" Jackson asked skeptically.

"I don't know. But in this kind of rock, there's a good chance we have plenty of chambers to work with."

"My size may be a problem," said Kadak!xa.

"I'm not worried," said Zeke. "We have sonar units for testing rock and estimating the size of chambers. With the ropes, clamps, and climbing tools, we'll do fine."

"And what do we do when we're deep inside the cave and at the end of the line?" Jackson demanded. "Make tea for them?"

"Ha, ha. I'm betting we can find another passage to the surface. This rock is laced with caves, and the whole cliff is big. Come back here and take some of this."

Jackson backed toward Zeke, still firing. "It's still a risk. You sure it's worth it?"

Zeke tossed him some equipment with a grin. "Kadak!xa, you first. If you can fit through a passage, we all can."

"If you want," she said, "I can hold them off here for you and then surrender."

"Nothing doing. You go and we'll cover for you."

"Zeke, I will limit the options you have—"

"I'm also worried about damage to the artifacts in this cave," Zeke said. "Come on."

Zeke moved forward again and resumed firing. The enemy had moved forward since he had last looked. If Kadak!xa remained here, she would be forced to surrender soon or risk dying anyway. Neither would accomplish anything.

Jackson rejoined him across the cave. They continued to fire, again watching the enemy slowly spread out and advance.

After a few moments, Kadak!xa called to them.

"We have a good passage here," she said. "I have enough space and firm footing."

"You first," Zeke said to Jackson.

Jackson fired twice more, backing away, then turned and hurried to the back passage.

"It's good, Zeke! Come on!"

Zeke paused long enough to pick out one rock he had seen earlier. It was fairly large, sitting above a slide of other rocks on the slope. He concentrated sustained fire on one spot until the rock cracked, broke, and began to roll.

The rock was too low on the slope to cause a major slide, but the rocks below it did begin to move. The slide fanned out and the enemy underneath the slide ducked and ran.

Zeke indulged in a grim smile and jogged back to the end of the chamber.

Chapter Eleven

Zeke had to hope that the small rockslide would slow down the enemy for a few minutes, at least. They would also have to approach the cave carefully in case they were walking into a trap. That gave Zeke some time to follow Jackson.

The first passage was just barely large enough for Kadak!xa to pass. In fact, as Zeke switched on the spelunking lights at his forehead and wrists, he saw the scrapes where she had forced her way past some loose dust and rock in the wall.

Ahead of him, Kadak!xa was releasing a sonar mapping unit to test the composition of the floor of the chamber. It was in the shape of a crab with bat wings and transmitted data to a modified earphone that was clipped to her head. This chamber was narrower than the outer chamber but nearly as high. Jackson was sonar-testing one wall with a similar unit. He and Kadak!xa moved forward slowly, as the crabs told them it was safe and fluttered to another spot before crawling along it for another sounding.

The crabs were also recording the route according to altitude and rock characteristics. With that data, they could find their way back if necessary.

Zeke waited anxiously at the entrance to the outer chamber with his weapon ready. He did not dare look out, lest he be seen. By the sounds he heard, the enemy was still moving up cautiously and had not reached the terrace of the cave yet.

"Okay, Zeke," Jackson whispered.

He and Kadak!xa were at the far end of the chamber, where they had tested two more branching passages. Kadak!xa was carefully easing into one of them. The other was too small for her.

Zeke joined them, still listening for the enemy. When he heard the first footsteps scraping on the terrace outside, he crouched against the wall and trained his laser on the opening. Behind him, Jackson followed Kadak!xa.

As soon as he could, Zeke backed into the passage after Jackson. The enemy would be entering the cave now in force. It would only take them an instant to realize where their quarry had gone.

Their commander would have to decide whether or not to follow and how many people to assign to pursuit. With luck, they would have to bring equipment over from the looted cave. All of this would slow them down even more.

Zeke turned and looked around the new chamber. It was low, very wide, and damper than the previous ones. As Kadak!xa moved forward slowly, her head lamp illuminated several large passages, all of them big enough for her to enter. No matter which one they chose, the enemy would have to consider all of them.

When the crabs had sounded all the walls and the floor of each passage, Kadak!xa and Jackson chose the safest one and the trio continued to venture deeper into the cliff.

Zeke would normally have never risked some of the passages and chambers they entered without more equipment. With rope, the sonar units, nose clips connected to oxygen belt packs, and lights fastened to their bodies, he felt they could afford certain risks under these circumstances. He had to distract Chrysanthi's crew from its duties and generally make trouble for them in the hope that he could later take advantage of their confusion.

They had passed through five chambers. The first two had been roughly level. The next two descended slightly, and the third rose, all of them with a trickle of water running in the bottom. More of the alternate passages they had passed were also large enough for them to have entered, leaving their pursuit with a multiple trail to follow on the rock floor.

Tracking equipment using heat sensors or even a Chrysanthi employee with a trained eye could have tracked them through the caverns. Apparently neither one was available. The one tool they would have in the looted cave was sonar equipment similar to Zeke's.

It could detect the vibrations of the fugitives as they walked, talked, and crawled. Fortunately, it could only tell them where the vibrations were, not what route would lead to the spot. As the enemy advanced, their position could be revealed the same way.

"I don't hear anything, Zeke," said Kadak!xa, as one of the winged crabs crouched on the cave wall. This time she meant sounds of the enemy behind them, not sonar for testing the chambers and rock. "You think they turned back?"

"I hope they took a wrong turn again," said Zeke. "But I'm not sure they'd give up this fast, especially if someone reported our identities to Chrysanthi himself—if he's in the Thomsen system personally."

"No kidding," said Jackson. "He would have ordered them to grab us at all costs."

"Any sign yet of an upward passage?" Zeke asked. "Our best chance to get out is to find an opening to another cave in the cliff, preferably one higher than the others."

"Or an opening to the top slope of the bluff," said Jackson. "Near the lander."

"Bad news, Zeke," said Kadak!xa. "I have two passages we can take, but they seem to rejoin later."

"So it's really just one," said Jackson.

"And it goes down rather steeply for some time." Kadak!xa gave a slow shake of her big hood, making the lamplight swing back and forth in the dark chamber. "We can go back or go down."

"Kadak!xa," said Zeke. "You use more oxygen than we do. How's your level so far?"

She looked down at the unit on her belt. "Fine."

"We should have plenty of oxygen in this system of caves," said Zeke. "The problem is ventilation. There's no air flow to speak of except for what our own movements cause. So keep careful track." He nodded to them. "Go down, then."

This was the most dangerous passage yet. It was low and narrow with a sliding gravel floor. The crabs had told them that the chamber was big enough for all of them, but they could not tell them how big the next passages out of it would be, or if any existed at all.

Zeke found himself sliding down wet gravel and rocks on his back, struggling to keep his feet from hitting Jackson's head and shoulders right below him. The chance of having to crawl back up this slide out of a dead end seemed good. Then suddenly they spilled into a large chamber, and Zeke lay on his back, looking up.

This chamber was only about four meters across, but it was very high. The walls angled in to darkness above them. Outcroppings in the walls blocked their lamplight from reaching very high. One passage led beyond the chamber.

Jackson and Kadak!xa began testing the chamber. Zeke was looking at the walls of the cave. They were unlike the others he had seen in the previous chambers during their descent.

He got to his feet and moved close to a wall so that his headlamp shone directly on it. The wall was light brown with sedimentary strata running up at a sharp angle. He turned and looked at the shape of the entire cavern.

This chamber was not a limestone cave at all. It was an opening created by the partial overthrust of sedimentary layers, where they had happened to trap softer rock and soil that had since been leeched out by water. These layers were similar to the ones they had seen exposed on the cliff, but were much older. In addition to the partial overthrust, they were different in having less damage by erosion.

Some clearly defined fossils were evident, many of considerable size. Zeke did not have a soft brush or anything else he could use to clear the surrounding material. Instead, he had to be content with blowing away loose dust.

The illumination from his headlamp revealed what appeared to be fossilized lupoid bones.

"We may have trouble here, Zeke," said Jackson. He pointed to a spot in front of him by one wall.

"What's wrong?"

"I have a couple of descending passages over here but they're borderline in size."

"You sure?" Zeke was still looking over the fossils.

"And I don't think we want to risk leaving the surface any farther behind."

"I have solid wall here," said Kadak!xa, from the other side. She swung her headlamp around the walls, looking.

"Zeke?" Jackson said. "You listening to us?"

"Sure," said Zeke. "Keep looking."

"Keep looking," Jackson muttered.

Zeke moved closer to the wall, examining details.

According to the fossil record, lupoids had lived in this area for a very long time. Many of the other fossils, of course, must have been prey or other predators. In some strata, Zeke found remains that were almost certainly Arr skeletons. They were the right size and their shape strongly suggested that these individuals had walked upright.

He could not find any forepaws to reveal whether or not they had had opposable thumbs. That would have convinced him they were Arrs. He had no frame of reference for estimating the age of these strata.

In the same strata, he also found some smaller lupoid remains. These creatures had definitely walked on four legs. Like the primate cousins of humans on earth, they had been contemporary, non-sentient relatives of the Arrs.

Zeke started to look at another level for older fossils, then stopped. He looked up at the entire wall. Since these layers had been thrust out of position by geophysical forces, he had to be careful in judging them.

On closer examination, he was certain that these layers had been reversed. Older layers were above later ones. Radiation and chemical dating could tell him a great deal more about them, and not just their age.

Obviously, that would have to wait. As he studied the adjacent layers, he found few differences in the fossils there from those in the layers he had just examined. Much of the rock, of course, did not have visible fossils.

He looked up into the dark recesses at the top of the cavern. Those were the oldest layers in this chamber, and he had no way to reach them now. If they journeyed deeper into the ground, however, they might find older layers that had not been overthrust.

"We've found what there is to find, Zeke," said Jackson. "Let's move on."

"All right." Zeke glanced at his oxygen level. "Let's try one of those passages."

Jackson turned to look at him. "I vote we go back up that rock slide and try another passage."

"Agreed," said Kadak!xa.

"I want to go down again," said Zeke.

"I still do not hear our pursuit," said Kadak!xa. "They are either off our trail or at least far behind."

Zeke shook his head, causing the beam on his headlamp to jiggle crazily across the walls. "If we can get down one of those passages, we're going."

"Zeke, that's crazy," said Jackson. "We're in a question-able spot already, if you ask me."

Zeke walked over and shined his lights at the openings Jackson had found. "We've come down passages that small before. Or close to it, anyway."

"I do not believe we are in imminent danger of capture," said Kadak!xa. "We should be safe enough back-tracking a little bit."

"That's not why I want to go," said Zeke.

"What?" Jackson demanded.

"I'm on to something here. We have a fossil record that may be worth a great deal."

"Fossil record!" Jackson laughed derisively. "Okay, we know where it is now."

"I said this was important." Zeke bristled.

"All right, Zeke. We'll come back for it after we save the Arrs from total destruction. Sylvie can come down and record everything properly. Till then, what's the point?"

"I'm going down," said Zeke. "If you want to get to the surface first, I'll meet you at the lander. Give me one of the sonar units." He held out one hand.

Jackson and Kadak!xa looked at each other. Neither one offered a sonar unit.

"Let me see if I can get down there," said Kadak!xa. She moved toward them.

Zeke and Jackson made room for her.

The passage to the next chamber was small but much of the rock and soil around it was loose. Kadak!xa opened her maw and began munching on the loose rock.

Jackson glanced at Zeke, who shrugged.

Kadak!xa ate her way forward and eased into the opening. Part of the way down she raised her hood to look up at them.

"Well?" Zeke asked.

"I've tasted better." She moved on down.

As before, Jackson followed and Zeke entered last. At this point, he hardly needed to act as rear guard against the enemy, but the Chrysanthi bunch might find them yet.

They entered this chamber on a descending slope, but it was firm rock, not gravel. The chamber itself was smaller and only about two meters high. Jackson and Kadak!xa began sounding the walls again, but Zeke admitted to himself that at first glance this did look like a dead end for them.

He glanced at his oxygen again. They had a long way to go to reach the surface by any route and a firefight with their pursuers could delay them further. When he was finished here, they would have to start for the surface.

"You looking for something in particular, Zeke?" Jackson asked, pausing to watch him.

"Yeah. Iridium-bearing clay or something similar."

Kadak!xa spoke quietly. "I have vibrations above us. They are faint, but present."

Jackson's jaw tightened. "They're still following us, then," he whispered. "Zeke, we don't want to be trapped in this chamber. The only way out is the way we came in."

Kadak!xa watched one of the winged crabs fly to another spot. "I doubt they will attack us if they realize we aren't fleeing. They will wait for our oxygen to give out instead."

"This is a small chamber," said Zeke. "It won't take me long to check everything here."

"You said you're looking for iridium-bearing clay?" Jackson asked. "Or something similar?"

"I want a sedimentary strip that holds more iridium than the surrounding layers," said Zeke. "Even if it turns out to be a difference in the parts-per-million range when we have it analyzed. It's the most likely mark of the last major cometary bombardment."

Jackson nodded as he picked up a recalcitrant crab and set it down on another spot. "I remember now. The layer represents the settling of dust after the comet smashed itself to a cloud of powder on impact with the planet. Right?" He was still keeping his voice low.

Zeke nodded, shifting his attention slightly lower. "It will be a thin stripe of color in the sedimentary rock."

"Sounds to me like that could easily be missed without better equipment."

"That's true," said Zeke. "The thickest layer of iridium on Earth is only a millimeter or so thick."

Jackson was right. He was looking in poor light under the necessity of haste. Nor did he have the sensing and analyzing equipment he normally would have carried.

"Our pursuit is slowly coming closer," said Kadak!xa. Then she took away the crab she was using and thumped on the wall of the chamber lightly.

"Ha! Jackson, look at this," Zeke said excitedly. "This might be the iridium layer."

Jackson joined him. "Where is it?"

Zeke pointed to a line of slightly darker color than the surrounding rock. It wavered crookedly, but spread in a direction roughly consistent with the sedimentary strata. "What do you think?"

"I wouldn't know what it is, Zeke. But I can vouch that you've found something here." He hesitated. "Let's go. We can come back here later, like I said."

"Not yet." Zeke squatted down to examine the strata under the line of iridium. A sharp pain shot through his stomach. He ignored it.

"There are no other openings to look for," said Jackson sourly. "We're trapped."

Kadak!xa was still taking readings.

Zeke had plenty of fossils in front of him. None of them, however, was what he sought right now. He began to move sideways, looking for more at the same level.

"This is it, Zeke," said Jackson urgently, holding his crab to another wall.

"What?" Kadak!xa asked.

"They're coming our way," said Jackson. "Listen to them yourself. Zeke, if we're going back up to find another way out, we have to get going *now*."

"Not yet." Zeke had found something else that might be lupoid fossils. They were close to the Arrs in size. He had to find more of them to be sure. Another stabbing sensation hit his stomach, probably induced by stress.

"Perhaps we should begin," said Kadak!xa. "Jackson, I will go first again."

Zeke was not listening. He had found the real object of his interest. "I have a layer of early lupoid fossils here," he said. "Almost certainly forerunners of the Arrs."

"Zeke, have you totally lost your mind?" Jackson growled, trying to keep his voice low. "Come on!"

"They were even larger in stature, though. If they walked upright . . . this could be the find of the entire planet." He pressed one hand surreptitiously against his abdomen.

Kadak!xa was struggling to move up the inclined rock floor of the passage. The largest part of her hooded head was well into it, but she was having trouble maneuvering in the confined space. She started eating an outcropping in the wall.

Jackson watched her anxiously, flexing his fingers.

Finally the enemy was so close that Zeke heard them with his naked ear. It was distant, not so much a specific sound he could identify as a faint thump on rock. A scraping sound followed it and what might have been a muffled voice.

Kadak!xa was nearly through the passage.

"We didn't have much luck in the last chamber, either," Jackson said through his teeth. "We'll go back as far as we have to."

"I'll follow you," Zeke said without looking up.

Jackson hesitated. When Zeke finally glanced up, he wondered if Jackson was about to grab him bodily. Jackson only turned, however, and started up the passage.

Zeke had found a couple of partial skulls. From their shape, he felt the forebrain of this specimen might well have been sufficient for a sentient species. He had to keep looking.

Above him, the sounds of Kadak!xa and Jackson moving about came through the rock. They were probably starting out of that chamber and into the one above it—that would be the gravel slide, difficult to ascend.

Zeke found a portion of a spine, but could tell nothing from it. Its length was not revealed in the surface rock. This fossil would have to be dug out carefully someday by someone with full equipment and time for the job.

For the first time, then, he heard shouts through the rock from above. He could not distinguish the words, but the enemy must have recognized its quarry. The abdominal pains had grown stronger and more frequent; now he knew this was the onset of the recurring infection he had carried since his days with the Legion of Ares.

The time had come for him to go. Perhaps he had taken too long for nothing.

Chapter Twelve

Zeke fumbled in his belt packs and found an emergency capsule he carried for these metabolic failures. It contained substances that would help him digest food but it would take at least an hour to have an effect and he would have to eat more food after that to gain any nutrition. He swallowed it.

More sounds reached Zeke from above. There were just thumps and scrapes, nothing he could identify. He knew he should go. With a determination to get back here somehow, he turned away from the specimens.

Just as he stood up, the beam from one of his wrist lights flashed across another section of rock near the floor of the chamber. White shapes in the rock caught his eye. After the other finds here, he couldn't just walk away. He looked closer, grimacing from the pains in his stomach.

Another skull was partially visible here. He trained one of his wrist beams directly on it, only vaguely aware of more sounds from above. Another spine was present here, nearly a whole one—and a pelvis with the lower portion of spine attached. This might be what he needed. He could not leave these unexamined.

Zeke knelt again and trained his lights first on the pelvis attached to the spine. His heart was pounding with excitement that had nothing to do with danger above.

From the shape of the spine and the pelvis and the angle at which they connected, he surmised that this specimen had walked upright.

He quickly ran the light over other fossils, looking for leg bones. They could have told him more, but he could not find any here. He did locate forepaws—or hands. The delicate little bones were detached and broken on the specimens in front of him, but he felt certain that opposite thumbs could be reconstructed out of them.

Zeke stood slowly, even more reluctant to leave the rich find behind than he had been a moment ago. Still, he had delayed longer than he had ever intended. He turned away and started up the passage into the next chamber.

The pains were becoming less frequent. That meant his attack was moving to the next stage. His body had already failed to metabolize the food he had eaten earlier that day; he would now be getting light-headed and weak from low blood sugar.

Low blood sugar itself did not cause his stomach pains, of course; they were caused by the accumulation of the virus in his stomach. However, he knew from past experiences the order in which he would feel each symptom.

When he had climbed up the incline, he found Jackson and Kadak!xa both poised at the entrance to the passage they had used to enter this one. A spray of gravel lay between them where it had fallen when they had come down.

"Decide to join us, Zeke?" Jackson said. "They aren't moving down toward us to get clobbered in this little tunnel. We had a little parley a minute ago."

"What did they say?"

"We refused to surrender, so they're just going to wait for our oxygen to run out."

Kadak!xa nodded. "We can surrender now or later. Or we can try to fight our way out and risk getting killed in the process. I do not see any other choice."

"Those fossils are as important as I thought," said Zeke. "Worth every moment down here." He glanced around the chamber. This was the first one formed by the overthrust layers of sedimentary rock, the one with a high-angled ceiling.

"Oh?" Jackson said. "As long as we're just waiting to suffocate anyway, you mind telling us what the big deal is?"

Zeke noted the sarcasm and chose to ignore it. "Something very rare happened on this planet, or at least I believe so. I don't have the data to be certain."

"Wonderful." Jackson shook his head.

"I think intelligent lupoids existed here prior to the last major catacylsm." Zeke was casting his wrist lights around the chamber, though he knew that the other two had thoroughly sounded the walls on their first pass through here.

Kadak!xa was listening with some interest. "Intelligent lupoids lived here before?"

"And if they existed very long, they may even have attained a fairly high level of cultural sophistication. I admit I haven't found any evidence of that yet."

"What about it?" Jackson asked, more soberly.

"I think that species of lupoid was made extinct by a cometary winter represented by the iridium-bearing layer I think I found. They left small, non-sentient cousins behind."

"Small lupoid cousins," said Kadak!xa. "You mean a species of lupoid small enough to survive on the small herbivores who lived through the cometary winter."

"That's right," said Zeke. "The small herbivores in turn were able to survive by eating whatever plants were able to grow while the dust cloud from the comet was in the atmosphere."

"And this small species of lupoid evolved into the current species of Arrs," Kadak!xa concluded. "That is your hypothesis?"

"So far," said Zeke. "And that's a far cry from other examples of planetary cataclysm. On Earth, the dinosaurs gave way to the evolutionary supremacy of mammals."

"All right, all right," said Jackson. "We get the picture, Professor Bones. But if we die down here, someone else will have to discover the fossilized remains of the whole bunch of us. Now what are we going to do?"

Zeke had finally looked up. The beam from his forehead lamp cut into the darkness above them. "We haven't checked up there yet. Let's see what's up there."

Jackson and Kadak!xa followed the beam of his light. The uneven cave walls threw shadows that obscured the area where the slanting walls came together.

"Worth a try," said Jackson.

"I'll watch the passage while you get into position," said Zeke. He moved aside to let them pass.

Kadak!xa found a spot near the center of the chamber and lowered herself to the floor. Then Jackson climbed gently onto the curve of her massive shoulders. As she slowly rose, he was able to hold on to her in a crouching position.

Zeke turned away from them long enough to pick up a handful of gravel. He tossed it up the passage. No return fire came down, but he heard boots sliding on the rock floor above as the enemy came alert at the sound. He grinned to himself.

Kadak!xa was still rising. As Jackson rose with her, he was able to reach out and touch one of the walls that angled in toward the center of the chamber. He braced himself against it to keep his balance. When Kadak!xa had reached her full height, he was able to stand and place the sonar sensor against the wall.

"See anything?" Zeke said.

Jackson shook his head. "I don't hear anything useful either." He let the crab fly to one side and land to try again.

Zeke looked at his oxygen level. It was low but not yet dangerously so.

Kadak!xa saw his motion and checked her oxygen also. "I don't have much time left."

Zeke nodded.

"Move to your left," Jackson instructed.

Kadak!xa complied. Jackson looked over a different wall and had the crab fly to it.

"Zeke," said Jackson, holding out a hand. "Toss me a rock hammer, will you?"

Zeke pulled one of the few tools they had brought out of his belt and tossed it up to Jackson.

Jackson drew the hammer back and struck the wall with a resounding *ping*.

Zeke winced at the sound. The enemy would certainly know they were doing something. There was no way to prevent it.

Jackson hit the wall again. The same sound resounded in the chamber. Finally, on the third strike, the hammer hit with a dull thud and bits of rock and dust fell on Jackson's face and shoulders. He turned and spat.

"What is it?" Zeke asked.

Jackson shook his head, motioning for quiet and pointing to the passage where the enemy waited. Then he reached one hand up into the hole he had made. He had broken through a thin layer of rock to another chamber.

Zeke didn't want their pursuers to figure this out and find another route to that chamber first, if there was one. To distract them a little, he tossed another handful of gravel into the passage and fired a weak laser burst into the gravel slide. He didn't shoot any more for fear of causing a rock-slide that would trap them.

A similar laser blast came back down the passage. They didn't want to cause a cave-in either. At least some of them would keep their attention on this passage.

Jackson had hammered the hole larger.

"Kadak!xa," said Zeke softly. "Can you get up there if it leads to a way out? If not, we might as well surrender."

"I cannot see up there without twisting around," she answered. "Jackson would fall."

"Give me one more minute," said Jackson. He had widened the hold considerably, causing big chunks of rock to fall and in some cases bounce harmlessly off Kadak!xa's massive back and shoulders. Now he put both arms up into the hole and started to pull himself up.

His head and shoulders were out of sight. His legs swung back and forth with the effort as his powerful arms and shoulders did all the work. Slowly, he moved up into the chamber overhead.

Kadak!xa raised herself up to look when Jackson was no longer relying on her. She studied the opening and its height for a moment. "I am still hungry," she said. "And I believe I can reach that level. I foresee no problem."

"All right," said Zeke, with a grin.

Several scraping sounds came from above. Then Jackson's smiling face appeared in the hole, just barely visible in the shadows. "Get up here if you can," he whispered.

Kadak!xa again lowered herself for Zeke to climb on her shoulders. When she was in position waiting for him, he fired one more shot up the passage. Then he hurried to Kadak!xa, virtually ran up her back, and jumped with both arms extended upward.

Jackson reached down to clasp wrists with him. Then he raised Zeke up until Zeke could brace himself on the floor of the new chamber. Zeke rolled out of the way.

As Jackson signaled for Kadak!xa to come up, Zeke shined his lights around the new chamber. It was extremely narrow but very high and steeply angled. The sides were like those below, partially overthrust sedimentary layers steeply angled.

Kadak!xa stretched up as high as she could, extending her segments to the extreme. When she had braced herself against the walls, she slid up into the opening. Jackson backed away so she could feel for a grip. When she had moved up against the narrowest part of the opening, she began chewing away the rock and soil to widen it.

Zeke and Jackson both sought out holds on the sides of the chamber. As Zeke watched, the thin, brittle floor cracked and broke upward. Kadak!xa continued to pull herself up until nearly the entire floor had fallen away or been devoured, the other pieces sliding off her head and shoulders. When her head was almost level with Zeke and Jackson, she spoke.

"I will hold on as long as I can," she said. "But I am very low on oxygen. Is there a way out of this chamber?"

"There's an excellent chance of it," said Zeke. "Do you see what this is?"

"Yeah," said Jackson. "It's an extension of the chamber below, going up."

"You might say it's all one chamber," said Zeke. "That little floor separating the two was just leftover soil and soft rock that hadn't been leeched out by water yet."

"It's a chimney climb," said Jackson, shining his lights upward. "It may go to the surface itself."

"If not," said Zeke, "it at least has a huge surface area. We may find another way out somewhere along the way." He felt for a hold and started climbing.

The chimney climb was narrow enough so that they could reach both sides of the chamber. They braced themselves wherever the best holds were found as they ascended. Kadak!xa had a very tight fit in several spots but was able to eat her way through any difficulty she met.

Suddenly a beam of light shined past Zeke from below. Instantly, he aimed his laser down past Kadak!xa and fired a quick burst. He saw the enemy for the first time since retreating from the outer chamber as they dodged away.

"Keep going," he said to the others. "I'll cover."

He remained where he was, with both feet and one hand securely braced. From here he was able to look down through the ruins of the floor Kadak!xa had demolished into the chamber below. He fired every time he saw movement of any kind down there.

Kadak!xa's movements seemed slow and careful. Actually, her segments were so long and powerful that every hoist of them raised her a good distance.

"Your turn, Zeke," said Jackson. "I've got a clear shot below so I can cover you."

Zeke stashed his weapon and began to climb again, now following Kadak!xa. His head was swimming and his body sweating heavily. In the bad light, the others had not noticed anything wrong yet.

"Just don't slip," he told Kadak!xa lightly. "If you go down, you'll take me with you."

"How about a raise, Zeke?" Kadak!xa answered.

Zeke forced a grin despite the effort of climbing. "We'll discuss it if I live long enough."

Jackson fired another couple of quick bursts to the bottom of the chamber.

The enemy was obviously not eager to return the fire. Any damage they did firing upward could bring a rock fall or cave-in on top of them. Zeke's party had to be careful, but they were in a better position now . . . as long as they found a way out.

Kadak!xa continued to climb, still forcing her way through several tight spots.

When Zeke had reached another firm position for himself, he stopped to cover them while Jackson climbed again. Alternating this way allowed Kadak!xa to climb without stopping. At one point, when she was far above them, she called down.

"Zeke, Jackson. I have an opening here to the side." She was looking into a shadow.

"Can you get through it?" Zeke asked, looking up.

"I think so."

Zeke began to climb again but was too weak to pull himself up.

"Zeke, you coming?" Jackson said. "I'm covering you."

Zeke pulled with his arms again, pushing off with his legs. His feet slid weakly on the uneven footholds. "Problem, Jackson. I don't . . . have a lot of strength."

"You *what*—" Jackson started, then paused. "Zeke, is it that metabolism problem kicking up?" His tone had changed to one of concern.

"Yeah," Zeke panted. "Afraid so."

"Catch your breath. We've got you."

Zeke closed his eyes and tried to get his breath back. He could hear Jackson climbing back down for him. Small bits of dirt and pebbles bounced off Zeke and fell past him. A moment later two large, strong hands gripped him under the arm and lifted him bodily upward.

"I can help— " Zeke muttered, reaching for a hold somewhere.

"Quiet," Jackson ordered softly.

Zeke could see Kadak!xa pushing sideways into the shadows above them. Her segments stiffened with tension while her great body swung precariously overhead.

A moment later she was disappearing into a passage in the side of the chamber wall.

Jackson reached up into the new chamber with one hand, braced his feet against the opposite wall of the vertical climb, and somehow hoisted Zeke up past him in the narrow space. Zeke wriggled his head and shoulders into the chamber after Kadak!xa. "Okay," he wheezed.

Jackson pushed him farther into the chamber until Zeke was safely inside.

When he could, Zeke moved around and looked down at the floor of the chamber they had left behind as Jackson began to climb again. A few of the enemy were still there to keep an eye on them. Zeke suspected most of them were moving quickly to the surface.

No one knew where Zeke and his companions would come out, including them. Sentries would still be waiting for them outside the cliff, watching all the cave openings they knew about. If the enemy was lucky, they might still intercept somewhere under the ground.

Zeke was still watching below, but he had not seen any of the enemy for some time. He backed up to make room for Jackson.

If the enemy had seen Kadak!xa disappear into the opening in the wall, that would explain their absence. They knew Zeke's party would not be coming down the same way. Right now, they would be using their sensors to estimate where Kadak!xa's passage would lead.

Kadak!xa had moved down the chamber to release a sonar crab.

"How does it look?" Zeke whispered.

"Don't know yet," Kadak!xa answered.

Zeke looked around with his lights. His spirits rose as he realized it was another limestone cave. It was almost certainly part of the bluff that ended in the cliff.

This part of the bluff rested against the overthrust layers that formed the tall, narrow passage they had just negotiated. He did not understand exactly how because the geological history of this planet was still unknown. At the moment he really didn't care about that either.

What was important now was the fact that the limestone caverns formed catacombs that gave them a good chance of getting out. Even now Kadak!xa was moving into another opening at the far end of this passage. He and Jackson were able to rise up into a half-standing position to follow her.

As soon as Zeke had followed them into the next chamber, he could feel the difference. A breeze was blowing against the sweat on his face. He and Jackson grinned at each other.

"There," Kadak!xa said quietly, looking upward.

The ceiling of this chamber was about three meters above her head. Zeke could see a tiny hint of light indicating the outside. It was too small to send any light into the chamber.

Kadak!xa began to rise up, pushing her head slowly into the opening.

Jackson began taking readings on the chamber wall. After a moment he looked at Zeke. "They're a long way off. If we get out in time, they won't have any more noises to listen to."

"And they won't know where to pick up our trail," Zeke finished. "Good."

Bits of rock and dirt fell onto Kadak!xa as she manipulated the opening to the surface. Then she turned to the others. "It is now big enough for one of you to look out."

"I'll reconnoiter," said Zeke. "I need the fresh air. Hoist me.

Kadak!xa lowered her head for him to climb on her. Then she raised him up. He put his hands together, arms stretched over his head, and pushed through the opening.

Zeke shoved aside sod and twigs. By the time he could support himself with his arms, his head and shoulders were over the sod. He seemed to be somewhere in a lightly forested part of the bluff.

He looked around, disoriented. Finally, in the distance behind him, he recognized the portion of cliff that held the cave openings. Just enough trees and brush stretched from him toward the cliff to cover them if they were careful as they climbed out of the opening here.

Zeke pulled himself out all the way and rolled to the side of the hole to keep low to the ground. Then he wriggled back to look down at Kadak!xa's upturned face.

"Come out, but stay as low as you can," he said. "We aren't far from the cliff."

Kadak!xa first boosted Jackson out of the ground. Then she pulled herself out, again smashing out the ground around the opening to make room for herself as she rose. All three of them then lay close to the ground looking around.

"Well?" Jackson said to Zeke. "Now what?"

Chapter Thirteen

On board the *Ostrom*, Sylvie swiveled her chair away from the console to look at Marty.

"Are you getting anywhere?" she asked him hopefully, knowing that she was interrupting him.

"Mm, well, not to speak of," he muttered without looking up. He frowned at the information in front of him and looked at Sylvie plaintively. Then he shook his head.

"What's wrong?"

"The *Ostrom* simply doesn't have the power or weapons or anything else that can be used to move that comet out of its path," he said. "It's that simple."

"Are you in the mood to take a break?"

"I don't see what good that would do." He shrugged his broad, solid shoulders. "How is your work going?"

"I really don't have very much to work with. We can't get any more word about Peter Chrysanthi's activities." "And you've finished going through the data about him we have stored here?"

"Yes, just now." She was watching him, unable to stop a playful smile from giving away her mood.

"What is it?"

"Well . . . Marty, are you up for a little adventure?" She tossed back her hair, making her jewelry jingle.

He studied her for a moment, his solid, full features unexpressive. "I'm still following Zeke Bones around the universe, aren't I? What's on your mind?"

"I've found Chrysanthi's ship."

"Really?" He straightened with interest. "How did you get through those invisibility shields?"

"I didn't, exactly," said Sylvie. "But our sensors were able to pick up a lander they sent down to the planet. In fact, it's gone back and forth a couple of times since we've been here."

"On a regular schedule?"

"Yes, and I had the computer record its path and follow it back to give me the position of the big ship."

"Well, well . . . Maybe we do have enough to work with. Could you pick up their orbit?" Marty asked.

"Their orbit is slightly higher than ours and out of sight on the opposite side of the planet. But I've had the computer speed us up very slightly. For the last hour or so, our ships have just barely been in sight of each other." "Haven't they noticed?"

"Not so far," said Sylvie. "Every so often they drop the shields for a second or two."

"Any idea why?"

"No, not for sure." She glanced at her console screen again for the data there.

"You have a guess?"

"Well . . . my guess is that some of their sensors are limited, perhaps jammed, while those shields are up." She shrugged. "Maybe they drop them at regular intervals to see out, you might say, as they scan the planet or communicate with their landing party."

"Can you intercept their transmissions? Is that what you're getting at?"

"No. Their transmissions are coded in a way we can't read. But it seems to me that we might just get on board Chrysanthi's ship somehow. For instance, I know when the lander is due to return next from the surface."

Marty's hard features slowly stretched into a grin. "I don't see how, but . . . it sure would break the monotony." "And it could get us some critical information about Chrysanthi's plans."

"So how do we get aboard?"

"I have our ship sensors recording the intervals at which they drop their shields. If we're careful, we can fly the unwinged lander right up to them between intervals."

"But how do we get inside?"

Sylvie grinned. "That'll have to be your department, Marty. But I've also recorded the transmissions their lander uses when it approaches. What do you say?"

"I thought you said you couldn't break the code." he cocked his head to one side.

"I can't, but I know it's the same transmission every time. We can make some use of it, don't you think?"

Marty gazed in her direction, but she knew that he was thinking and not really seeing her at all. "I'm not sure of the details yet," he said slowly. "But I think we can take a shot."

"Let's do it, then. The *Ostrom* can stay on automatic for the short time we'll be gone."

Marty hesitated. "I don't think Zeke wants the ship unoccupied. Maybe if one of us stayed—"

"We won't tell him," said Sylvie.

"Not tell him—"

"Until afterward," she added. "After all, you'll need my sensors and recording equipment, and I need your expertise to get inside their ship. All right?"

"All right." He shook his head but he was grinning. Sylvie turned and started looking over the data she had on the Chrysanthi ship and its position.

"The intervals during which the Chrysanthi ship is both invisible and mostly blind are just barely long enough," she said. "If we're lucky and very precise, we can fly the lander from here to there without being seen by them."

"It's worth the risk," said Marty. "If they see us, I think they'll just run. That's been their pattern."

"Let's go."

Sylvie flew the lander while Marty considered the possibilities for sneaking aboard. They took off right after the Chrysanthi ship went invisible to the *Ostrom*'s equipment and flew on the most direct route to intercept its position. As they drew near, however, they were faced with the problem that their target was still invisible.

Marty took control of the grappling cables. They were firm but flexible extending cables with electromagnetic clamps on the ends. Marty extended them to maximum length and Sylvie started a painfully slow approach in the direction of the Chrysanthi ship.

"They're about to drop their shields again," said Sylvie. "Their sensors will detect our presence here for sure if we don't get inside their range."

"Careful, careful . . . Bring us in a little more," Marty watched his screen closely. Suddenly the clamps fastened onto something invisible in space.

A couple of seconds later, the Chrysanthi ship suddenly appeared over them on the screen.

Meanwhile, the lander was retracting the cables to pull itself right alongside the ship.

Sylvie tensed. "If they're going to see us at all, they'll see us right now."

"Hear anything?"

"No." She was turned into Chrysanthi's transmission frequency. "Even if I can't understand their coded communications, I'll know if they start a frantic exchange with their party on the planet."

"Will that be enough?"

"I think if they've noticed us, they'll start jabbering about it. If not, we'll just have to proceed."

"So far, this is what I was hoping for," said Marty. "We're now attached to their ship, in a sense, and their sensors probably have registered us as part of it."

"That will do."

"They'll notice us if someone looks carefully at the readouts, of course."

"But they aren't suspecting anything," said Sylvie. "So what do we do now?"

"How long till their lander is due to return?"

"About thirty minutes, if they're on schedule."

"All right." Marty climbed out of his seat. "Time for me to get into a pressure suit."

Marty climbed into his suit, one tailored to his powerful, massive body and oversized hands and feet. He had rigged several kinds of sensors to magnets on the trip out. All were prepared both to record and transmit back to the lander on signals from Sylvie.

"We're cutting the time short," said Sylvie. "I have to send this signal close enough to their schedule so they aren't suspicious, and early enough for us to get out of here again before their lander shows up and see us here."

"I'm ready," said Marty. "Let's just hope they're still operating on automatic." He finished fastening the helmet of his suit.

Several moments later, Marty was out of the lander's airlock, propelling himself with a small handgun of compressed gases. In his other hand, he carried a longer gun of the same sort with a magnetic dart in the barrel.

He floated slowly along the hull of the big ship toward the closed entry their landers used.

"Ready," Marty said through his helmet's communicator. Sylvie had kept him on the lowest power possible to avoid Chrysanthi's crew picking up their conversation. Avoiding unnecessary talk was best, of course.

A moment later, he heard the transmission Sylvie had recorded from Chrysanthi's lander as she played it back. This was also at a low volume. He could detect a variety of tones, and knew that a complicated pattern of inaudible frequencies would also be included.

The entire operation depended on the next moment. He watched the closed entry, waiting. Finally, just as he was about to give up, it began to slide open to admit their lander.

Marty moved to the edge of the open airlock and looked inside. He had only a few moments before someone would realize that their lander was not entering the hangar. Without time to look around, almost any place was as good as another. He hooked his knees around the edge of the opening to brace himself.

Marty took careful aim with his long compressed-air gun at an interior wall of the hangar. He picked a spot near a ceiling corner, hoping the sensor would go unnoticed there. Then he fired.

The dart flew relatively straight, though his makeshift dart was hardly a precise match to this gun. As he had planned, the magnet clamped the sensor to the wall. He fitted another dart of the same sort into the gun and looked for another spot.

"Red alert," Sylvie said briefly but firmly in his helmet.

That meant the real opposition lander was on its way. They would have to hope that the Chrysanthi crew just thought the premature opening was a malfunction. Certainly, if they were suspicious they would find the sensors.

Marty fired the second dart up high, to hit just inside the frame of the door. Then he turned and propelled himself as quickly as he could toward the safety of their own lander.

He slipped inside the lander again and took his seat. As he unfastened the helmet and slid it off, Sylvie put her hand on his arm and nodded toward the viewscreen. The enemy lander was moving into position almost next to them.

"What do you want to do?" Marty asked.

"They could have seen us," said Sylvie. "They may be alerting the big ship now."

"If so, this was for nothing," said Marty sourly. "They'll sweep for bugs."

"We'll play possum," Sylvie decided. "I think there's a good chance this procedure is so routine that they're letting the computers do it all. Alone out there, you were just too small to attract attention. If the computers are running on automatic, they won't notice us unless we trigger their computer alarms by running away."

"Fair enough. We'll run for it after they're inside." Marty sighed. "What kind of sensors did you give me, anyway? Can you really get anything worthwhile off an airlock wall?"

"Hard to say," said Sylvie. "It'll pick up all kinds of things—engine hum, footsteps, intercom talk, casual conversation. It'll be a blur to the naked ear."

"Huh?"

"The computer will do the real work."

"How so?"

"The computer on the *Ostrom* can sort it all out," said Sylvie. "It can lock onto a certain voice, amplify it, and give me the entire sentence. If some words are still unclear, it can give me some probable words to fill into the context."

"Not bad."

"Naturally, it will pick up best from the lander and the airlock itself. If people say the right stuff in the right places, we'll get it." Sylvie held up crossed fingers.

"We can hope," Marty nodded approval.

"I'll have the computer process all the human speech we get and discard the other noises. I can also tell it to kick out every mention of Thomsen 4, comets, Dr. Bones . . . anything pertinent." She turned to her console.

"So now we just get back to the *Ostrom* and wait."

"Right."

In several moments, the enemy lander was inside the big ship. The entry door was closing again. Even before it shut all the way, the Chrysanthi ship vanished from Sylvie's screen.

"Time to go," she said simply, and hit the controls.

When they returned to the bridge on the *Ostrom,* Sylvie found her console lights blinking brightly and quickly. It could only mean that Zeke was calling. She hurried over to it.

"*Ostrom,*" she said briefly.

"Sylvie!" Zeke shouted. "What's wrong?"

"Everything's fine, Zeke."

"What happened? Why weren't you answering?"

"Uh . . . well, we may have a new source of information if it works out," she said, glancing at Marty.

"Sylvie." Zeke's tone was threatening. "Answer me. What have you two been doing up there?"

Marty patched in at his seat across the bridge. "We bugged Chrysanthi's ship, Zeke."

"You *what?*"

"We planted two bugs on his ship. And I don't think we got caught, either."

"Without telling me?" he demanded. "I thought we'd been boarded and captured!"

"It was . . . a rush job," said Sylvie.

Zeke was silent a moment. Then Sylvie heard his distinctive laughter. "All right, all right. Just so it worked out okay. The details can wait. Have you picked up anything worthwhile?"

"Not yet," said Sylvie, sighing with relief. "It hasn't been very long. We can't decode their surface-to-ship transmissions, but we'll get all kinds of loose talk from on board. We just have to wait till the right conversation comes along."

"Understood," said Zeke. "Listen, Sylvie, I just wanted you to know that you'll have plenty of data to record down here when the planet is safe."

"Really? What did you find?" Sylvie asked.

"A treasure trove," Zeke said enthusiastically. "Arr cultural artifacts, fossils, caves where they and their ancestors have lived for years—and I mean in the millions. The odds against stumbling across it are impossible, but we did."

"Murdock did the real research," said Sylvie. "She dropped Calvin at the most likely spot to find what you found. It wasn't totally an accident."

"I stand corrected," said Zeke. "Anyway, we have to preserve this planet."

"I'm not sure we'll manage that," said Marty gruffly. "I haven't come up with anything."

"Do it," Zeke insisted. "This planet may have some unique features in its history of evolution. We *can't* lose it."

"I can't change the laws of physics," said Marty. "Or the time we have available."

"Marty—"

"If you can change either one, then do it," he growled angrily and broke contact.

"You know, Zeke," Sylvie interjected. "Nobody put that comet into orbit. This is a natural disaster. I don't mean it won't be a tragedy, but no one's to blame."

"Chrysanthi's to blame," Zeke declared. "Without him, Murdock would have diverted the comet."

"We'll do what we can," said Sylvie. "But if we can't do it, no one can. We can't solve every problem in the universe."

"We'll take them one at a time," said Zeke. "Right now, this is the one. Tell Marty to stay on it." He broke contact.

Sylvie looked at Marty.

"Zeke Bones can be very persuasive," said Marty. "His confidence can be contagious. But you can't change the laws of physics with a silver tongue."

Sylvie nodded sympathetically.

Anything that could be accomplished with skill, daring, intelligence, or even financial backing was within the realm of their team. The invariance overdrive even defied ideas once thought to be inviolate. However, she agreed with Marty on the impossibility of this problem. It was just too simple. They had to push a big comet, and had nothing to push it with.

Marty was sitting slumped back in his seat, staring at a viewscreen. From what she could see, it was aimed away from Thomsen 4 and the Thomsen sun. It showed only points of light against an unending background of space.

Sylvie knew better than to interrupt him. His apparent stargazing was for the purpose of meditation, in a sense, or a private brainstorming session. He was probably seeing comets colliding with planets over and over in his mind.

Suddenly a line of information appeared on her own screen. She turned to find that the computer was kicking out data from the bug on Chrysanthi's ship, as she had instructed. The first line was raw data. She skipped down to the lines enhanced by the computer analysis of the data and then to the conclusions.

"PETER CHRYSANTHI HAS PLACED NUMEROUS BETS REGARDING THE COLLISION OF A COMET WITH THOMSEN 4."

"Details," Sylvie ordered.

"ALL BETS VIEW THE COLLISION AS A NATURAL EXPERIMENT IN EXTINCTION AND SPECIATION AS FOLLOWS: THE COMET WILL HIT THE PLANET; ALL INTELLIGENT LIFE WILL BE DESTROYED; SOME ANIMAL LIFE WILL REMAIN; THE SURVIVING FORMS OF LIFE WILL HAVE A CERTAIN MAXIMUM WEIGHT..."

The list went on.

Chapter Fourteen

Zeke took his party deeper into the forest, away from the bluff. He did not want to stop during daylight because their pursuers might still pick up the trail. They rested briefly, two at a time with one person on a rotating watch. Zeke was able to consume some of the rations they had been carrying once his capsule had taken effect and he felt his energy begin to return.

For the time being, Zeke was hoping that their lander had not been found. He saw no point in returning to it, since Jackson had camouflaged it as well as possible. If it had been found, a trap might be waiting for them there anyway. If necessary, Sylvie could eventually pick them up in the other lander.

The one totally unpredictable danger was the Arrs. Zeke had no idea where the Arrs were or what their attitude toward them would be. No Arrs appeared. Whether or not they were watching them from the forest in secret was another matter.

When night fell, Zeke finally relaxed. The Chrysanthi group had higher priorities than finding him. They also possessed no greater knowledge of the terrain than his party. He knew they would not pursue him through the forest at night.

The Arrs could appear at any time, but Zeke saw no point in worrying about it. They could do nothing to avoid or to defend themselves anyway. The Arrs were at home here.

Zeke and Jackson consumed more of their rations. Kadak!xa was already full. She found a place for them to sleep beneath a tree fallen against a large rock. The supplies Zeke had requested for the cave included thermal belt units that did not give off light. They had not been intended for use in the open air, but they made the cool night a little more comfortable. Compared to some of the conditions during Zeke and Kadak!xa's service in the Legion of Ares, this night was not bad at all.

The first light that filtered through the trees awakened them. They had not slept long, as the Thomsen 4 night was short during this season, but Zeke did not dare stay in one place any longer. They consumed another limited portion of rations and started out.

Zeke led the way with careful reconnoitering and a slow, cautious advance. They picked their way through the forest to a spot where they could again see the various cave mouths in the cliff. The Arrs were still mysteriously absent.

Since emerging from the ground, Zeke, Kadak!xa, and Jackson had taken a long, circuitous route away from the bluff. It had led them back into the forest that Zeke's first landing party had initially crossed. That was when they had followed the path from Calvin's lander to his cave in the cliff. Now, after sleeping in the forest, they had circled back to approach the cliff from the same side again, though without the benefit of a path to hasten the way.

When they first peered through branches at the edge of the forest, Zeke saw considerable activity in the cave where they had first met Calvin.

"They're just starting their day," said Jackson. "Have they finished looting here yet, do you think?"

"Possibly," said Zeke. "Look."

As they watched, a line of Chrysanthi crew members began carrying sealed crates out of the cave in a long line. They moved slowly, negotiating the narrow Arr path that led from the cave terrace down the base of the bluff to the forest. No lander was in sight, nor was one likely to be in the dense forest nearby.

"Their lander must be on one of those open hills in the forest," said Kadak!xa.

"Maybe the first one we landed on, or else somewhere close to Calvin's lander," said Jackson.

"That means quite a trek through the woods, doesn't it?" Zeke grinned at them.

"Zeke, we can jump them in the forest," said Jackson. "We'll have plenty of cover, and they're burdened with cargo. That can more than make up for the difference in numbers."

"For what purpose?" Kadak!xa asked. "To return everything to the cave?"

"Or to take them ourselves," said Jackson.

"Perhaps we should let them take the artifacts off the planet and then retrieve them through legal means. Marty has said he cannot divert the comet."

"Chrysanthi can sell everything on the black market long before we can get them back by legal means," said Zeke.

"No kidding," said Jackson.

"Besides," said Zeke. "Marty's a pessimistic grouch when he's working. He'll think of something."

"Shall we ambush them, then?" Jackson looked like he was ready to get started.

Zeke shook his head. "There's too much danger to the artifacts. I don't want them in the middle of a shooting gallery."

Jackson looked annoyed. "Then what do you want to do? Just stand by and watch?"

"For the moment, yes. Let's wait for them to start through the forest, and then follow them."

Jackson sighed and sat back.

Zeke estimated that about half of the Chrysanthi crew was carrying artifacts. Most of the containers were carried by handles between two people; a few were carried by one person. The rest of the crew remained in the cave, packing other containers.

He noted with satisfaction that they had not brought down any vehicles to help them on the trip through the forest. If Chrysanthi's ship had none, it meant he had not anticipated this find. In any case, carrying everything on foot would slow them down.

When the Chrysanthians had moved completely into the forest, Zeke led the way toward them. They were using the Arr path. Stealth was crucial, but the Chrysanthians were so noisy as they blundered through the forest that they were not likely to hear anyone else.

Zeke entered the path well behind the last bearer. Jackson and Kadak!xa followed him in that order. They were able to stay a good distance back and out of sight; the noise and trampled underbrush left a clear trail for them to follow.

Zeke was just stepping over a small rock in the path when shouts rose up from the Chrysanthians. They were followed by screams and cries that he remembered hearing from the Arrs. With a quick glance back at Jackson and Kadak!xa, he jogged forward carefully and pulled out his hand laser.

Around a corner, Zeke saw the bearers dropping their crates under a hail of spears, throwing axes, and arrows. The Chrysanthians had no compunctions about killing Arrs, and began to return fire with laser weapons on maximum. Zeke was horrified to see some of the Chrysanthi bearers ducking down behind crates full of artifacts for cover and shooting over them.

"Come on!" Zeke called to his companions. "Just don't hit those containers!" He knelt and took careful aim at the nearest Chrysanthi uniform. As he fired, Jackson and Kadak!xa joined him.

Zeke jumped out of the path behind forest cover, still firing. A short distance away, he saw a couple of Arrs with spears looking at him in surprise. Shifting his laser to a lower power, he turned to face them.

Alongside him, Jackson was still raking his laser rifle fire across the Chrysanthians. The Arrs studied him for a moment, then accepted him and his companions as allies. Both turned to heave their spears at the Chrysanthians, shouting and howling as they did so.

"I hope they're spreading the word to the others about us," said Kadak!xa.

The forest in the immediate area was catching fire in spots from the intensity of enemy laser fire aimed at the Arrs. The green forest did not burn easily, but the Arrs were clearly more frightened of the fire than the humans. They began to back away, still firing arrows and throwing spears.

From the slightly greater distance, the effect of Arr hand weapons was weaker. The enemy lasers were no less powerful and continued to drive back the Arrs. However, Zeke and his companions had put a number of Chrysanthians out of action at their end of the line. The others were crowding up the path to get away, bunching with their fellows in the narrow file among the scattered crates.

Zeke stopped firing and looked toward the sky. All he could see were the tall trees waving overhead. "Kadak!xa, Jackson."

Jackson looked up, too. "Yeah, I hear it."

"Me, too."

It was the sound of a lander overhead, approaching fast and coming down low.

Zeke dove deeper for cover, aware that Jackson and Kadak!xa did so at the same moment. They hadn't called the *Ostrom*, so it could only be a Chrysanthi lander. A moment later, screams and howls rose up from the Arrs—and Kadak!xa.

Zeke turned to look at her. The unseen lander was moving past overhead, probably to land somewhere nearby. Kadak!xa was rolling on her back, crushing bushes and saplings and smashing branches with her writhing tail.

"Sound?" Zeke asked, watching her helplessly.

She didn't answer right away.

Zeke turned and fired again.

"Yes," Kadak!xa said hoarsely, when she could. "My head is ringing from the vibrations." She stopped rolling and lay still for a moment, breathing hard.

"A high frequency, maybe," said Jackson. "Or some combination of vibrations. A weakness they discovered in the Arrs that doesn't bother humans."

"And it got me by chance." Kadak!xa rose, shaking her head ponderously.

Zeke turned and resumed firing. The Arrs were pulling back into the forest.

"Well, Zeke?" Jackson fired also, but glanced over his shoulder at the retreating Arrs.

"Well, what?"

"Are we going to retreat with them or go some other way? We can't hold this position alone."

"Kadak!xa, can you move out?"

"Yes, I can."

"Let's pull back through the forest. Try to keep some of the Arrs in sight."

Most of the Chrysanthians were staying on the path with their loot. A few who had started into the trees after the fleeing Arrs turned back after a few meters.

A few minutes later, all shooting had stopped. Zeke hurried through the underbrush, struggling to keep the Arrs in sight as they moved much more comfortably through the dense woods. Several of them had seen Zeke and his companions but none of them showed any interest in slowing down for them or communicating directly.

Zeke stopped, leaning one hand against the trunk of a large tree. "We can't keep up."

Jackson nodded, watching the Arrs vanish into the trees ahead. "I guess they don't want to talk to us."

"All right," said Zeke. "Back to the Chrysanthians, then. I suppose that lander came down to pick up the cargo and the bearers radioed that they were under attack."

They started back to the path. The Chrysanthi bearers had been joined by the crew from the lander. The newcomers were armed with laser rifles and were clearly out of breath from hustling along the path to reach the firelight.

Zeke and his party watched as the Chrysanthians tended their casualties and picked up their crates again. This time the lander crew formed an escort alert to signs of attack. When they began to move down the path once more, Zeke gave them a little more distance before following them.

They moved along the path for some time without incident. Then Zeke heard an isolated cry followed by shouts. A couple of laser weapons were fired briefly.

Zeke and Jackson looked at each other in puzzlement. They crept forward and then Zeke dropped to a prone position and wriggled on the ground until he could see.

One Chrysanthi man lay face down with a big Arr arrow in his torso. A couple of his companions were kneeling over him. One looked at the other and shook his head.

Zeke withdrew and silently formed the word "sniper" with his mouth to Jackson and Kadak!xa, pointing to the far side of the path. The Arrs who had fled had moved west; from the angle of the arrow, the Arr sniper was east of the path.

The Chrysanthians had gone only a few more yards when the incident was repeated with another bearer.

Zeke understood that the Arrs intended to destroy the enemy's morale this way and it was clearly working. He was surprised, however. The Arrs had not shown this much subtlety before. Their tactics had been no more than charging in a mob and then fleeing the same way.

As far as he was concerned, the Arrs themselves had answered all questions about their intelligence in the affirmative.

He was expecting the sniper attacks to continue. However, several moments after the second one, a chorus of howls and whoops filled the air up ahead. He hurried around the next bend.

The Arrs had sprung a trap. They were leaping on the Chrysanthians from tree branches, swinging down on them from vines, drooping woven nets over them, all the time screeching and howling in lupoid triumph.

Zeke, Jackson, and Kadak!xa once again focused their weapons on the end of the line. This time, however, the Arrs were clearly in the advantage. Many of the Chrysanthians were thrashing helplessly under nets, and the arrows and axes of the Arrs were more effective when used from above.

The Chrysanthi lasers were fired erratically, frantically, at the Arrs leaping down from above. Others remained hidden in the leafy trees to shoot their arrows almost directly down on their quarry below. Just as the Chrysanthians began to gain some composure, another rain of stone axes and throwing sticks descended on them. They had no cover from above.

"I think we're gong to take them this time," Jackson shouted over the Arr yells.

"I hope there's something left of the artifacts," said Zeke. He stopped firing for a moment. "Look."

To their left, the first Arr party was returning. They were trotting back through the forest with axes and clubs. Most of their throwing weapons had been expended in their first attack. Now, as the Chrysanthians were fighting hand-to-hand and firing anxiously up into the trees, the second party fell upon them on the ground with the same cries and howls as before.

"Hold your fire," said Zeke. There were too many Arrs on the trail to avoid hitting them.

Jackson and Kadak!xa stood alongside him on the trail, no longer concerned about return fire from the enemy. The Arrs had them surrounded and confined.

As they watched, the struggling suddenly stopped. A long series of howls rose up from the Arrs. The beleagured party had finally surrendered.

The Chrysanthians all stood motionless with their hands high. Arrs took weapons from their raised hands while shoving them and chattering and growling in their own language. Some of them began to lift the sealed containers with gentle reverence.

Suddenly Zeke saw a familiar face push forward into the crowd. It was Calvin, speaking in growls and other gutturals to the Arrs and pointing to the crates. The Arrs seemed to be listening to him.

"Come on." Zeke put away his weapon and started through the path, waving. "Hey, Calvin!"

"Zeke! Come over here!" Calvin grinned.

The Arrs parted, looking suspiciously at Zeke and his companions at first. More growls among them seemed to alleviate the suspicion, however, and Zeke briskly led the way to Calvin's side.

"They just had a crash course in military maneuvers," said Calvin, wiping sweat off his face. "And it worked."

"Good job," said Zeke, looking around at the scowling prisoners. "But what was that first attack by the Arrs for? That one didn't accomplish anything."

Calvin shrugged, still grinning. "They're intelligent, but they don't have any practice in coordinating maneuvers. They got overanxious and attacked too soon. Watching these crooks run away with their sacred symbols was too much for them and they couldn't wait."

"At least they came back," said Jackson. "Arrows and spears against lasers. I like these guys."

"They have no cowards among them," Kadak!xa agreed.

"Once I had begun to return the artifacts to the cave walls, I started winning the Arrs' friendship back," said Calvin. "It was tricky, but when the Chrysanthians moved into the cliff, we ran off together. That gave us a common bond."

"And then you planned this trap," Jackson finished. "Not bad for an anthropologist, Calvin. I'm impressed."

Calvin laughed. "Funny. Neolithic weapons and their use were part of my field training. It was *supposed* to be for observation and understanding. I never had to *use* it before."

The Arrs were watching and listening without understanding the conversation.

Calvin turned to the Chrysantian prisoners and pointed to the crates. "Return these to the caves where you got them. The Arrs will escort you. And remember, they're already mad."

"Hey," said one Chrysanthi man. "Aren't you coming? We can't even converse with 'em."

"I'm not coming," said Calvin. "I'll be busy going over the records you left in your lander. I want to find out everything you know about this planet. Better do exactly what they want, because you can't talk your way out of it." He winked. "And they are carnivorous, you know."

"That should take care of matters down here," said Zeke. "Now we have a comet to move."

"I've been thinking," said Jackson. "Suppose Calvin takes up one enemy lander and I take another. You and Kadak!xa can fly ours up. That will reduce Chrysanthi's resources."

"What about his crew?" Kadak!xa asked.

"We'll get them later," said Calvin.

"Calvin," Zeke began. "I know they're carnivorous, but—"

"The Arrs won't really eat them," Calvin added in a lower voice. "They may use them for additional labor, though."

"All right," said Zeke with a grin. "Back to the *Ostrom*, everybody."

Chapter Fifteen

"Nothing," Marty said sourly, "I've been over all of our records several times, and we just don't have anything we can use to knock that comet out of the way."

Zeke had just returned to the *Ostrom* and gone right to the bridge, stripping off his extra gear as he went. Now he shook his head and collapsed into a seat.

"Sylvie, see if you can still reach Corlissa Murdock," he sighed. "Maybe she's thought of something."

Sylvie nodded and got on it.

"Marty," said Jackson. "Axe we close at all?"

Marty shook his head. "I know several ways to do something like this. I just don't have the tools to do it."

Kadak!xa moved up next to Jackson. "How did Chrysanthi get involved out here in this system, I wonder?"

Sylvie looked up. "Apparently he came out here on a snooping expedition of his own, about the same time Murdock found the system. I think he was here a little earlier. They did their research independently, of course."

"And as a betting man, he saw one set of possibilities," Zeke observed. "As a developer, Murdock obviously saw another. Put that together and here we are."

"I see."

Sylvie turned to Zeke. "I got Murdock's assistant. They're trying to rendezvous with Calvin and get back to Earth. She still can't help us with the comet."

"I'm not surprised."

Jackson sighed and took a seat.

"Calvin's calling from the Chrysanthi lander," said Sylvie a moment later.

"Put him on the speaker," said Zeke wearily.

Sylvie did so.

"Zeke," said Calvin. "I have another problem to worry about. Thought you ought to know right away."

"Another one?" Marty demanded.

"Go ahead," Zeke smiled wryly. "What difference will one more make at this point?"

"This is crucial information for diverting the comet," said Calvin. "I've been reviewing the info here in the Chrysanthi lander. According to their records, Thomsen 4 occasionally has an aberration in its orbit caused by a planetoid that swings close by."

"A planetoid, too?" Zeke asked. "It figures."

"That's right. And if the comet passes near the planet when Thomsen 4 is on its orbital aberration, it might hit the planet, as we calculated, or it might just miss. If you divert the path of that comet without factoring in the aberration, you might make it hit the planet when it wasn't going to on its own."

"Not much chance of that now," said Zeke. "The truth is, we don't see any way to divert the comet anyway."

"Hold it right there," Marty called out. "What are you, Zeke, some kind of a pessimistic grouch or what?"

"Huh?"

"Calvin," said Marty. "Stow this talk and send up all the data you have, right away."

Zeke and Sylvie looked at each other and shrugged most simultaneously.

"Here it comes," Calvin said. "Zeke, it sounds like you have a decision to make."

"What?"

"I have an entire load of Arr loot all crated up. We had the prisoners return it to the cave pending your solution to the problem. But if you don't have one, I'll fly this up on the lander if the Arrs will let me . . . and I'll have to say goodbye to every last one of them."

Zeke stared at the floor for a moment, then looked at Marty.

"Sylvie," said Marty. "Distract everybody, will you? I have to concentrate." He swung his seat back to his screen and began to watch the data transmission from Calvin.

Zeke laughed, suddenly excited about their prospects for success again. "Calvin, stand by for as long as you can. The data you just gave Marty may make the difference."

"Corlissa is anxious to get back to Earth," said Calvin. "Don't take too long."

Zeke looked around. "Come on, everybody—off the bridge. Marty will call us when he's ready."

"Stay, Sylvie," said Marty. "If Calvin gets in touch again, you take it. I don't want to be disturbed."

"Okay."

Zeke shrugged and led everybody out.

The respite gave Zeke time to clean up and unwind a bit. The time for diverting the comet was growing short. He didn't know what Marty had in mind, but at this late date it would be their only chance. He stretched out on his bunk, wide awake, thinking about how all these events had come about.

Chrysanthi had discovered a possible collision between a comet and a planet, made chancy by the presence of a planetoid in the vicinity. True to his nature, he had seen the situation as a betting situation. Everything that followed had come from that one decision—the destruction of Murdock's business, the attacks on Zeke and his ship, the looting of the Arrs' cultural icons, and now Marty's effort to save the planet. It was, as he and Sylvie had discussed before, like one white cue ball hitting a set of racked billiard balls and sending them all flying.

He was too tense to relax. Time passed slowly as he pictured the disaster if they failed. Saving a few artifacts would be all they could do. The Arrs would be destroyed, and their evolutionary record possibly lost, depending on the details of the collision.

"Zeke," Sylvie said over the intercom at last. "Marty says he may have something."

Zeke leaped out of bed and returned to the bridge.

"Marty?" He called out briskly as he strode into the bridge. "How does it look?"

"It's going to be complicated, Zeke," said Marty. "Take a look at the calculations on my screen."

Zeke leaned over Marty's rocklike shoulder. "What do we have here, then?"

"That small planetoid Calvin told us about makes all the difference. Remember, the Thomsen System is full of them."

"That's what you have on the screen here—planetoids and their orbits?"

"That's right. Look, this one over here is small enough for us to push with the *Ostrom*. We can plant charges to steer it by exploding them in the right directions."

"Wait a minute. That one has been on our records all the time. Why didn't you figure this out before?"

"I did. Only before, it couldn't help us any. Look, it's too small to knock the comet aside by itself. What we have to do is steer it into a collision with *this* planetoid." He pointed to another one.

"Aha—and that one . . . ?"

"If those two combine, instead of bouncing off each other, the combination will be big enough to jar the planetoid that swings by Thomsen 4."

"To jar it? Meaning . . . ?"

"Meaning *that* one can divert the comet by hitting it, especially if it also carries the added mass of the first two sticking to it. You follow me all the way?"

Zeke whistled. "And the distances between them are right? That is, we have time to move everything into the right spot when it has to be there?"

"It'll be very close, but we might just make it." Marty nodded to himself looking at his data. "We might."

"Okay, Marty. This one is your show. You tell me what we need to do and I'll coordinate it."

Marty's solid, bulky features stretched into a rare full smile. "Exactly what I had in mind, Ezekiel."

Moments later, the *Ostrom* was racing out of its Thomsen 4 orbit toward the smallest of the planetoids in Marty's plan. Their course took them from the sun.

The details for the entire project were worked out during the trip. First, Zeke, Jackson, and Kadak!xa would plant explosives in certain spots on this small planetoid. When they went off, the rock would be steered out of its existing orbit.

Zeke and his team planted the charges successfully, working by hand in pressure suits, with Kadak!xa's huge arms doing most of the muscle work. Then they returned to the *Ostrom* and withdrew a safe distance before triggering the explosions in series.

Everyone watched on viewscreens as the charges exploded.

"Well, Marty?" Zeke asked, when the last one had finished. "Is it on course?"

"Seems to be," said Marty. "We'll have to follow it for some distance to get its new orbit exactly."

"I've been stalling Calvin," said Sylvie. "He's called a number of times and I kept saying you were involved in delicate operations."

"I was," said Zeke. "Put him on the speaker."

"Time's running short, Zeke," said Calvin. "Corlissa wants to go. Can you move that comet or not? Shall I try to rob the Arrs blind without getting dismembered myself? I'm not looking forward to it, but I don't want to lose these artifacts, either."

Zeke looked at Marty.

Marty grimaced at his screen for a moment, then shrugged apologetically.

"Can't tell yet, Calvin," said Zeke. "All I can say is that we're working on it."

"Great. I'll just sit here and keep smiling at all these fangs. Keep me posted."

Zeke grinned at Calvin's tone. "Marty, you and he should get to know each other."

The *Ostrom* followed the planetoid on its new course. At one point, Marty judged that it was slightly off its precise course.

The planetoid was actually light enough for them to move it slightly with the ship's power. Therefore, the *Ostrom* was able to make minor corrections as the planetoid drew nearer its point of collision with the next planetoid, a considerably bigger one. Zeke took the helm and with the computer's precise judgement brought the ship into gentle contact with the rough surface of the planetoid. One prolonged nudge from the *Ostrom* brought it exactly into Marty's specifications.

Soon enough, the planetoid was approaching its interception point. Again, Zeke and his team watched on their screens.

"Moment of truth," said Marty, as two points of light on his screen moved inexorably together. "If they don't hit each other, the Arrs are finished."

Several seconds later, only one point of light registered on the screen, moving in a new orbit.

Zeke grinned. "Marty, what about Calvin? Can I tell him it's okay to leave?"

Marty shook his head. "We have two more collisions to go. If anything goes wrong, you'll want him down there to bring up the artifacts—assuming he can get them from the Arrs somehow."

"Are we on schedule so far?"

"Yeah, but that new planetoid we've created out of the two that just collided is a little off course. I suggest hitting it with some missiles on one side. I'll tell you exactly how much fire in a few seconds." He started more calculations.

Zeke caught Sylvie's eye and motioned for her to leave the bridge. She nodded and slipped away.

"My turn," said Jackson enthusiastically. Everyone's mood was upbeat now. "I'll program the missile fire. What do you want and where do you want it, Marty?"

"It's coming on screen."

The *Ostrom* moved into position and began firing missiles at the misshapen planetoid they had just created by ramming the first two together in just the right way. Marty's calculations had included the mineral substances of all the planetoids as well as their momentum, so he knew exactly what material he was handling. If he was correct in his plan, this new creation of theirs could be steered into the path of the big planetoid that caused Thomsen 4's orbital aberration.

The missile fire stopped.

"Marty?" Jackson said.

"Not quite enough."

"Continue firing," said Zeke.

"We're out of missiles," said Jackson.

"*What?*" Marty looked up in surprise. "We're still slightly off course. We have to hit it with something."

Zeke looked at him. "We have lasers, particle beams . . . Jackson, what else is still on board?"

"They'll take too long," said Marty. "We have to hit it with something now."

"The Chrysanthi lander," said Kadak!xa. "We still have it in tow."

"Right!" Zeke turned to Jackson. "We'll send that crashing into the planetoid."

Sylvie was just coming back onto the bridge. "I hate to bring this up," she said, "but technically it's still the property of Chrysanthi."

"Write up an invoice," said Zeke. "For our expenses coming out here. If it hadn't been for his actions, most of this effort would have been unnecessary. We'll send it to him with the cost of the lander deducted from it."

"Right! Uh, what if it doesn't add up to the cost of that lander?" She asked.

"By the time you've added everyone's salary, it should. Come to think of it, throw in something for Murdock's extra expenses, too. And something for the Arrs, to cover the damage done to their caves. And anything else legitimate you can think of. The truth is, he'll wind up owing other people for this."

Sylvie laughed and got to work.

Marty looked up from his latest calculations. "That lander has enough mass, but we'll have to fly it into the planetoid at full speed to get enough momentum."

"Jackson?" Zeke said.

"I can set it to follow our computer signal if there's time." He started working on this console. "Okay . . . I have its computer . . ."

"Less than a minute left," said Marty.

". . . matching its frequency to ours . . . Okay!" Jackson looked up. "So any time you're ready, Marty . . ."

"Go to it."

Several minutes later, Zeke watched on his screen as the lander pulled away from the *Ostrom* and headed for the planetoid. As it flew, Jackson manipulated his console.

"On course," said Marty.

Everyone watched in silence as the point of light representing the lander flew closer and closer to the planetoid. Then it struck the larger body. It exploded in a flash that registered on other instruments as well.

"Perfect," said Marty. "Better relax for a while, folks. The next collision isn't due till later in the day."

No one relaxed. The day wore on and the planetoid now seemed to take forever to make its rendezvous. Zeke couldn't think of anything else and apparently neither could the others. They were all strangely silent, as if waiting for the next collision was the only event that held any interest for any of them.

At last the time for the collision approached. No one had to be warned. All of them were watching the time and they drew close to the screens on their own.

This time, the planetoid they had created was about to hit the one Chrysanthi's people had identified.

"Come on," Jackson muttered.

The two points of light edged closer and closer.

"I'm sure I calculated right," Marty said quietly. "But even the slightest error could throw it off—"

Sylvie jabbed him in the ribs with her elbow.

The points of light drew even closer.

"Now!" Zeke said, clenching his fist.

The points of light finally merged. The new combined body took a sharply divergent course from the previous orbits of the two planetoids.

Marty checked the new orbit and nodded in grim satisfaction. "One more smash-up, folks. Don't go away."

"How long?" Sylvie asked.

"Only thirty minutes till comet time," said Marty.

Zeke nodded to Sylvie, who turned and waved.

"Do you think Calvin can safely leave the planet now?" Zeke asked Marty.

"Yeah, I guess," Marty said reluctantly. "We could still miss the comet, but our chances are pretty good now."

"I'm glad to hear it," said Calvin, laughing as he walked onto the bridge.

"Calvin?" Marty blinked. "Zeke, what did you—"

"Easy, Marty. Just chalk it up to how much faith we have in you. I had Sylvie tell him to rendezvous with us some time ago. You were too absorbed in your work to see him coming in on the readout." Zeke laughed pleasantly.

"I wouldn't have wanted to try to get the artifacts away from the Arrs again," said Calvin. "Anyhow, they have the Chrysanthians hard at work cementing everything back into the cave."

Zeke extended his hand. "Congratulations."

"Why did you join us out here?" Kadak!xa asked. "We're a long way from Thomsen 4."

"Murdock had to return to Earth," said Calvin. "Sylvie told her I would ride home with you. I'm just glad that little lander got me all the way out here."

The time for the last collision approached. No one spoke. When no one was looking, Zeke crossed his fingers behind his back.

On the screen, the two points of light again moved closer together. They seemed to intersect, but they did not merge. After another few seconds, the two points separated, apparently having passed each other.

"Marty!" Sylvie wailed.

Jackson slammed a fist down on the console.

Kadak!xa made a strange rumbling sound and Calvin stiffened next to her.

"Marty?" Zeke asked quietly.

Marty was studying his console screen intently. At last he let out a breath and sat back in his seat. "No problem. They didn't stick to each other, but the planetoid struck a glancing blow off that comet that has changed its course. The planet is safe."

A chorus of cheers rose up, followed by Sylvie throwing her arms around Marty.

Jackson gave him a friendly cuff on the back of his head. "That's for scaring us all like that," he growled, mimicking Marty's voice. "Good job, Marty."

"Thanks, Marty," Zeke called over the ruckus.

"Zeke, we have a call," said Sylvie excitedly.

"Murdock?" Calvin asked.

"No—Peter Chrysanthi."

"Put him on speaker," Zeke said with a grin.

"Zeke Bones," Chrysanthi's voice screamed. "Bones, you rot-gutted, crater-pitted, space-frozen, laser-blasted, underhanded filthy cheating scum—"

"Turn him off again," Zeke laughed. "He must have been monitoring the comet, too."

"And he knows he lost big on all his bets," said Sylvie, breaking contact.

"All right, everybody," said Zeke. "Let's get back to Thomsen 4 and make friends for real with the Arrs this time. Oh, and one more item, Sylvie—"

"Yes?"

"Transmit that invoice to Chrysanthi right away and tell him the use of his lander was crucial in our diverting the comet. Thank him for me, will you?"

Chapter Sixteen

Back in the halls of New Yale University, Zeke strode down a corridor grinning to himself. Lois Thurman had open office hours for students at this time. He knocked on the door frame and leaned his head playfully into the open doorway. She was alone.

"Hi, Lois."

"Yes? *Oh*—" She paused in surprise.

"Mind if I come in?" He grinned.

"Can I stop you?" She smiled wryly and waved toward a chair in front of her desk. "I couldn't stop you from leaving, as I recall."

"Well, I *am* sorry about taking off on such short notice—"

"*Sorry?* She demanded. "For what—sticking me with nearly twice the lecture schedule I normally have and a class preparation I haven't reviewed in years? And for that you're just . . . *sorry*"

"Actually, I came to offer you something." He sat down.

"Like what? Lunch with the famous Dr. Bones? Do you think one lousy lunch can make up for all the hassle you dumped on me? Or maybe you brought me a set of salt and pepper shakers from an alien culture of arachnoids or something?"

"Not exactly." Zeke laughed. "Hear me out. I have a planet with a sentient species of lupoids and data suggesting some highly unusual developments in their evolutionary history. An anthropologist named Calvin Louie will be doing research in his field, but it's wide open for anyone else in any other area. The planet has just been opened up for long-term research. You interested in a year of sabbatical doing fieldwork?"

"Wow." Lois sat straight up. "Are you serious?" Her eyes narrowed. "Why would this other guy share his discoveries with me?"

"I'm sharing *my* discoveries with you. Anyhow, Calvin is a decent fellow and he knows he can't cover a whole species and culture alone, not to mention an entire planet. He'll work with you."

"Zeke, if this is a joke of some kind—"

"No! Not at all. A developer is going back there in a few months and will take you with her."

"A few months!" Lois sighed. "I really don't think the department is going to let me off in the middle of the year—"

"I spoke to Den Tanaka as soon as I got back," Zeke grinned at her. "It's already decided."

"It is?"

"As long as I agree to take over *your* current duties here."

"I . . . I guess I'm in shock. It's all so sudden."

"Tell you what, Lois. Put a sign on your door that you had to leave unexpectedly and . . ."

"And what?"

"Come have lunch with me."

"Lunch?" She started laughing.

"Correction," said Sylvie, appearing in the doorway. "Have lunch with both of us. Right, Zeke?"

"Uh—right, Sylvie." He turned back to Lois and shrugged. "I . . . *we* . . . will tell you all about the planet."

Lois stood up and shook her head. "Not exactly, Zeke. You can start taking over my duties now."

"What?"

"My office hours won't be over for another ninety minutes. You stay here in case students come in with questions . . . and I'll go to lunch with Sylvie."

"Hey, wait a minute—"

"Okay with you, Sylvie?" Lois asked, walking around her desk. "You can tell me all about the planet."

"Good idea!" Sylvie laughed. "See ya later, *boss* man."

Lois and Sylvie departed down the hall.

Zeke shook his head and collapsed back in his chair, laughing.

Visual Data By
JOEL HAGEN
Character Designs By
STERANKO

Dr. Bones is an outspoken proponent of the theory that cometary bombardment can have a profound effect on the pattern of evolution. In between missions, Bones devotes much time to field work and research on this subject. In addition, he often delivers lectures on the topic to his archaeology classes at New Yale University. The following data samples, taken from his personal computer files, have proved extremely important to the development of his argument.

When Dr. Bones heard about the impending collision between a comet and the recently discovered planet Thomsen 4, he was convinced that he had found the ideal circumstances for testing his theories. The data collected while exploring the caves of the planet, particularly the discovery of an iridium-rich layer, was just the kind of information he was hoping to find.

But there was a startling new twist: It had previously been thought that cometary bombardment causes drastic changes in the direction of evolution, saltations in which a totally different species gains dominance after the cataclysm. In Earth's case, for example, small mammals superseded the dinosaurs. But the fossil remains found by

Dr. Bones indicate that the evolutionary pattern on Thomsen 4 was dramatically different. The Arrs are collatoral descendants of a sentient lupoid race which had existed before the planet's first collision with a comet. No saltation was made. An analogous situation would be if an advanced species of chimpanzees evolved in the aftermath of the destruction of the human race.

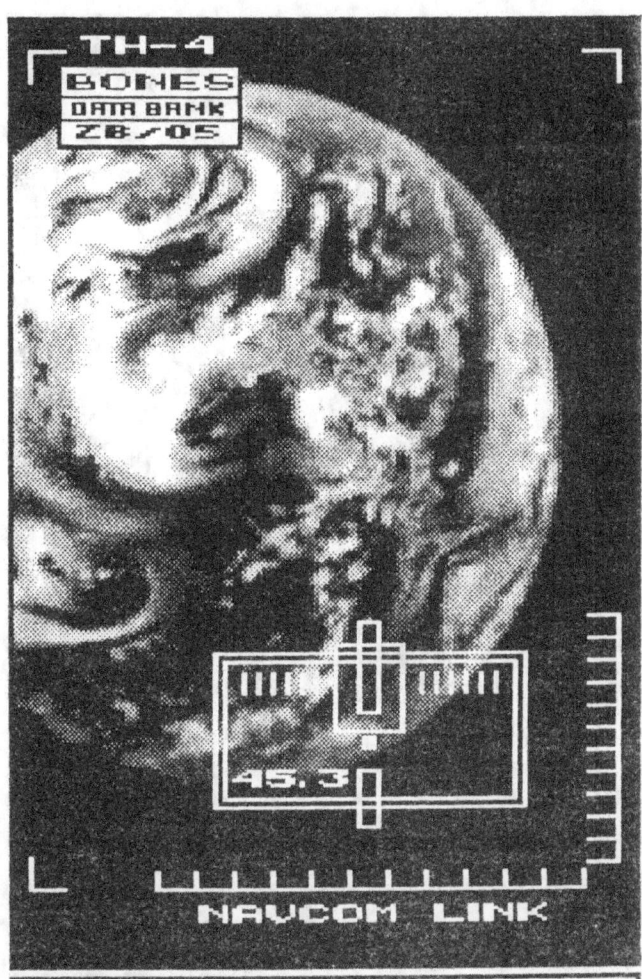

TH-4
BONES
DATA BANK
ZB/05

45.3

NAVCOM LINK

IMAGING SCREEN   BONES
THOMSEN 4 APPROACH

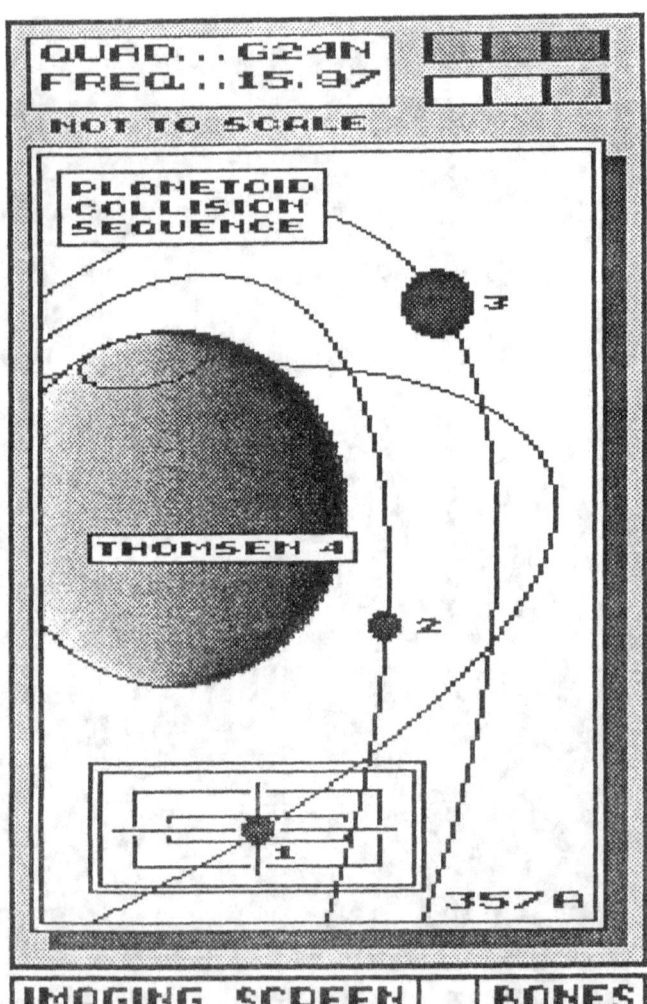

COMET
NAVCOM LINK

BONES
DATA BANK
ZB/05

NUCLEUS

IMPACT ZONE

IMAGING SCREEN | BONES
DEFLECTION ANALYSIS

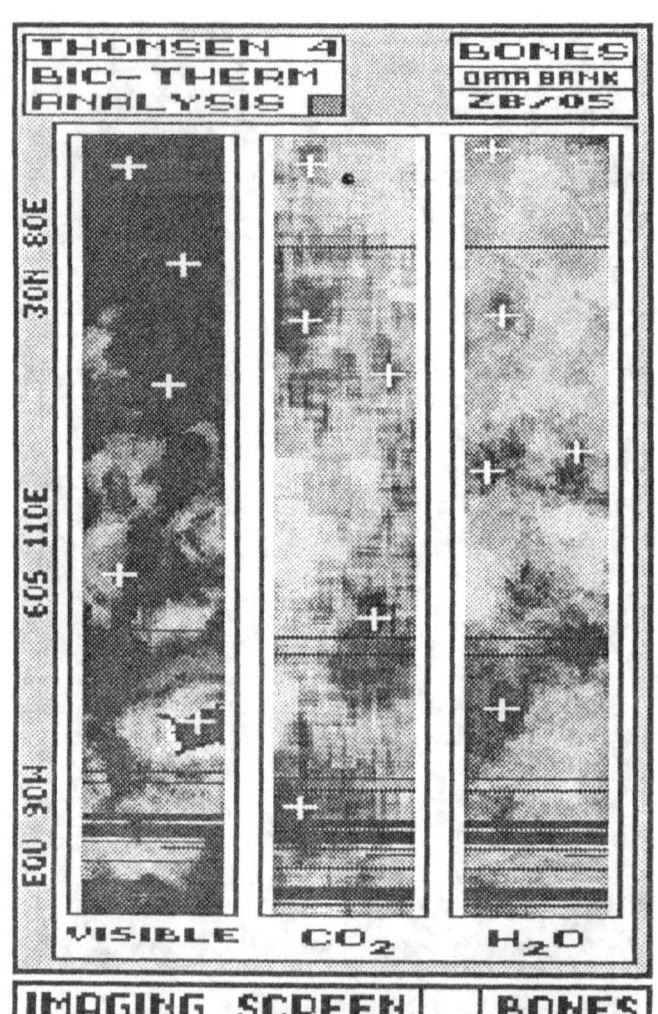

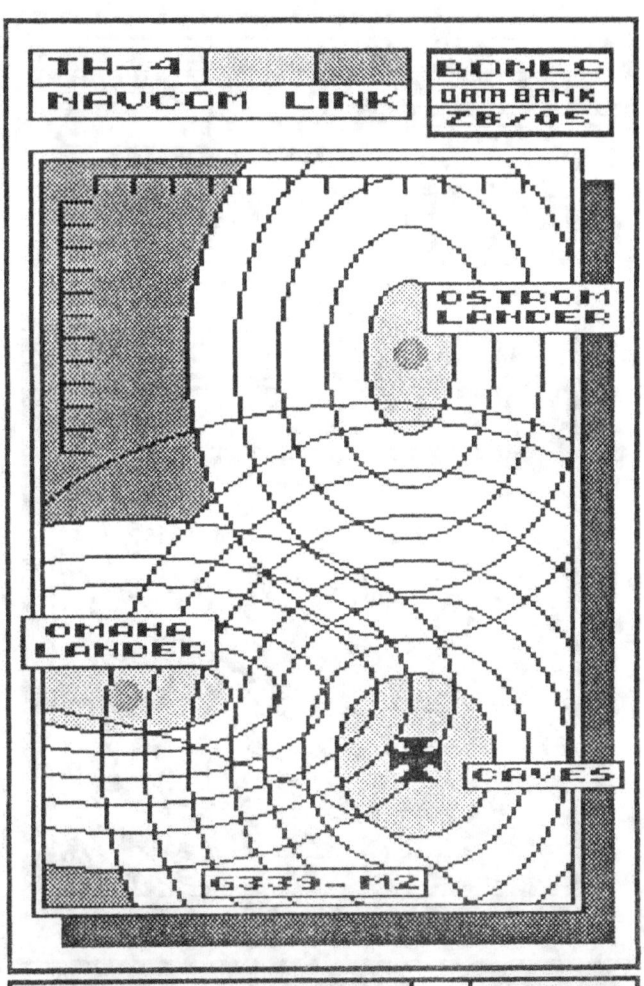

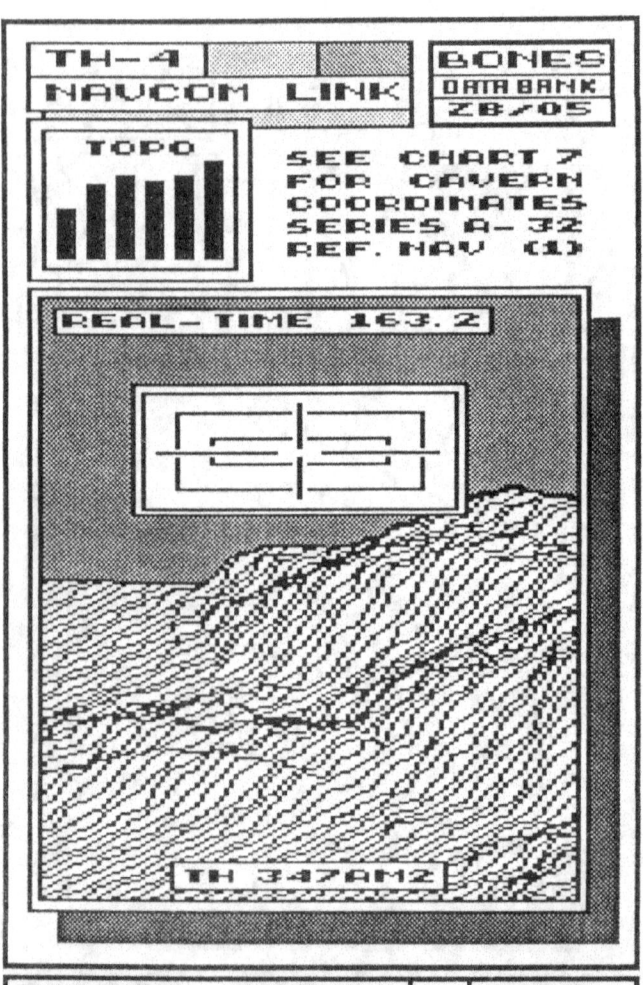

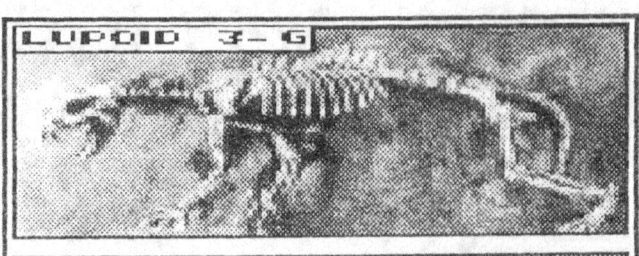

LUPOID 3-G

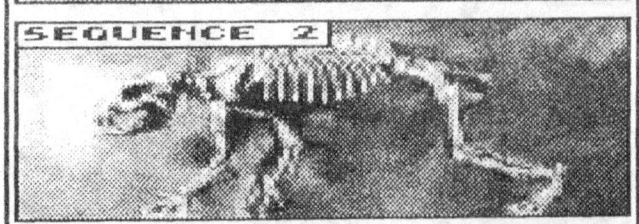

SEQUENCE 2

SEQUENCE 3

SEQUENCE 4

BONES
DATA BANK
ZB/05

FOSSIL EVIDENCE [F]
[B]

IMAGING SCREEN | BONES
ARR EVOLUTION

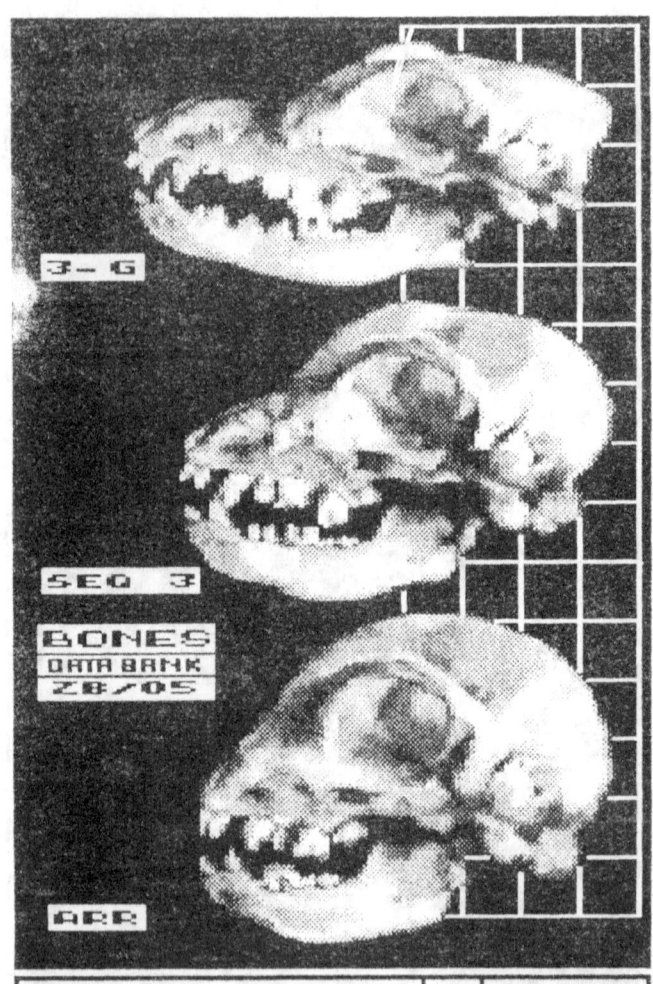

3-G

SEQ 3

BONES
DATA BANK
28/05

ARR

IMAGING SCREEN | BONES
ARR SKULL EVOLUTION

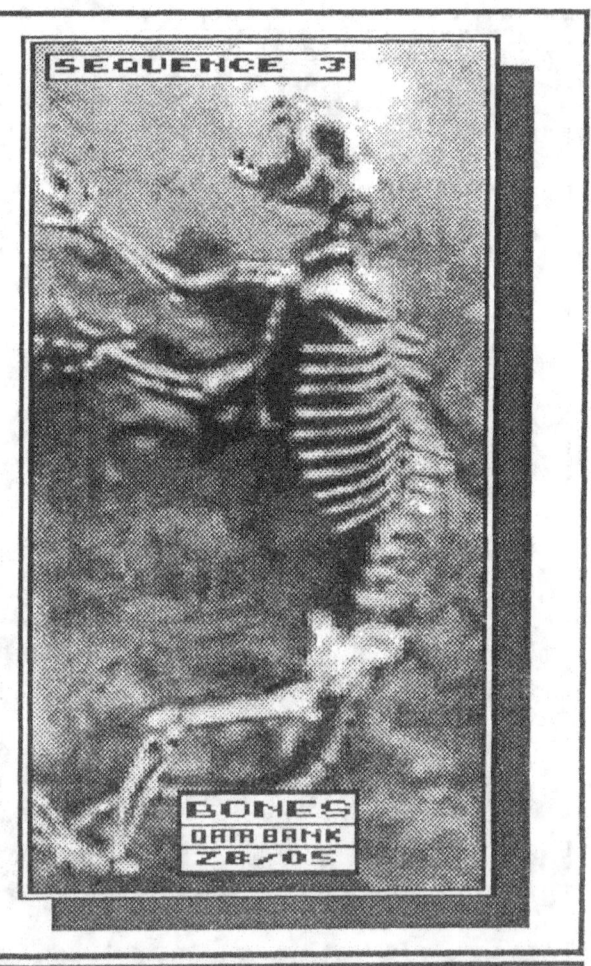

SEQUENCE 3

BONES
DATA BANK
ZB/05

IMAGING SCREEN | BONES
ARR ANCESTRAL FOSSIL

CAVE FIND B-29

BONES
DATA BANK
ZB/05

IMAGING SCREEN | BONES
ARR ANCESTRAL FOSSIL

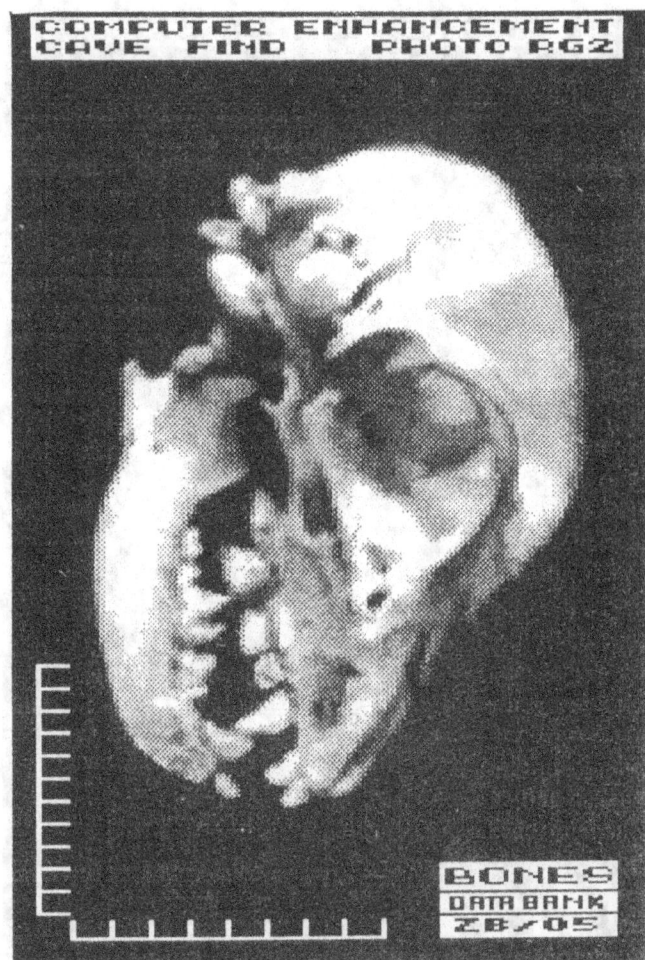

COMPUTER ENHANCEMENT
CAVE FIND   PHOTO RG2

BONES
DATA BANK
ZB/05

IMAGING SCREEN   BONES
SEQUENCE 3   ANCESTOR

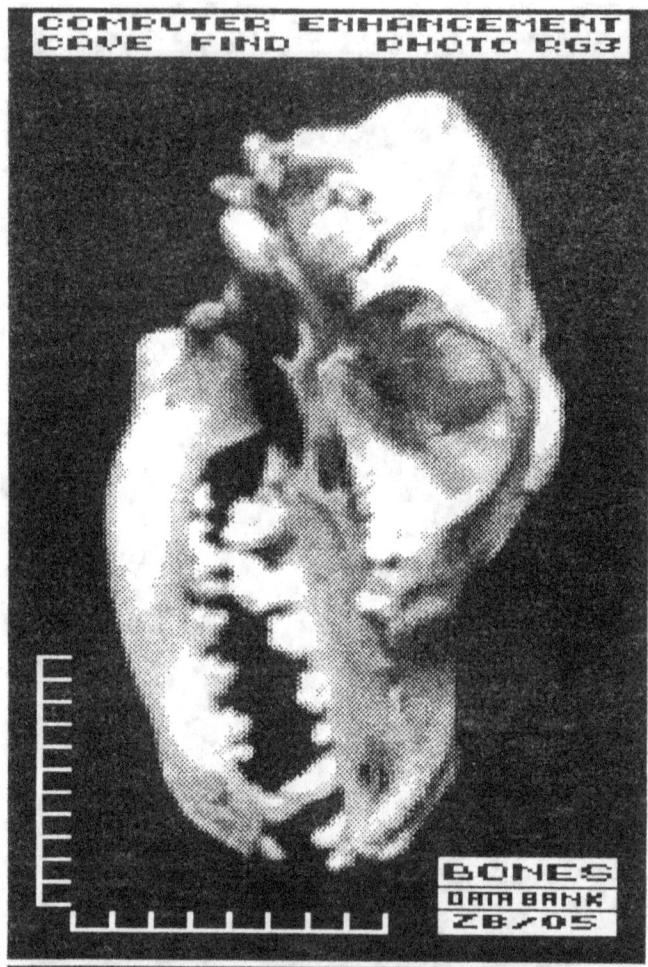

COMPUTER ENHANCEMENT
CAVE FIND   PHOTO RG3

BONES
DATA BANK
ZB/05

IMAGING SCREEN   BONES
LUPOID ANCESTOR

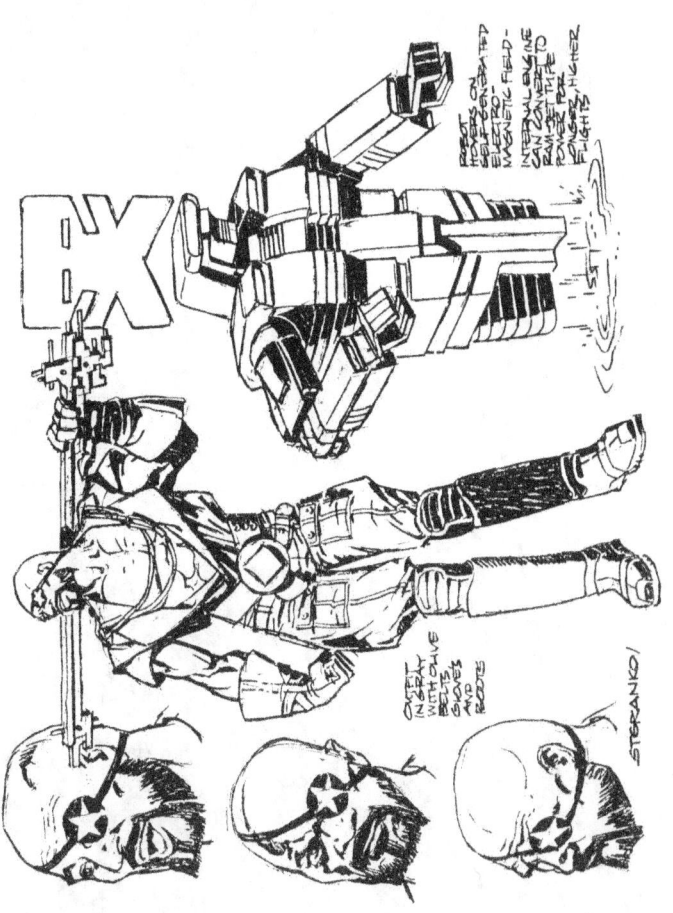